# Twice in a Lifetime

*A Small Town Second Chance Romance*

Second Hope Series

Jessica Prince

# Let's Connect

Let's Connect

By signing up for my newsletter, you're guaranteeing you'll stay up to date on all new releases, cover reveals, giveaways, sales, and all the other exciting book news I have coming!

I pinky-promise to use my emails for good only, not to spam you, and make sure each one is enjoyable for everybody.

Sign up on my website at: www.authorjessicaprince.com

# A Note from the Author

If you're curious about where Rhodes and Blythe got their starts, I've attached a little graphic below to make that easier for you.

brother of Gypsy in
WRONG SIDE OF THE TRACKS

daughter of Nona in
THE BEST OF ME

I hope you enjoy this story as much as I enjoyed writing it!

Happy reading, and all the love,
~ Jess

# Discover Other Books by Jessica

<u>SECOND HOPE SERIES</u>
*The Little Things*
*Tangled Up With You*
*Twice in a Lifetime*

<u>ASHLAND SERIES</u>
*Dead to Rights*

<u>WHITECAP SERIES</u>
*Crossing the Line*
*My Perfect Enemy*
*Turn of the Tides*

<u>THE PEMBROOKE SERIES:</u>
*Sweet Sunshine*

*Coming Full Circle*
*A Broken Soul*
*Should Have Been Me*


## WHISKEY DOLLS SERIES

*Bombshell*
*Knockout*
*Stunner*
*Seductress*
*Temptress*
*Vamp*


## HOPE VALLEY SERIES:

*Out of My League*
*Come Back Home Again*
*The Best of Me*
*Wrong Side of the Tracks*
*Stay With Me*
*Out of the Darkness*
*The Second Time Around*
*Waiting for Forever*
*Love to Hate You*
*Playing for Keeps*
*When You Least Expect It*
*Never for Him*

<u>REDEMPTION SERIES</u>

*Bad Alibi*

*Crazy Beautiful*

*Bittersweet*

*Guilty Pleasure*

*Wallflower*

*Blurred Line*

*Slow Burn*

*Favorite Mistake*

*Sweet Spot*


<u>THE CLOVERLEAF SERIES</u>

*Picking up the Pieces*

*Rising from the Ashes*

*Pushing the Boundaries*

*Worth the Wait*


<u>THE COLORS NOVELS</u>

*Scattered Colors*

*Shrinking Violet*

*Love Hate Relationship*

*Wildflower*


<u>THE LOCKLAINE BOYS</u>

*Fire & Ice*

*Opposites Attract*

*Almost Perfect*

## CIVIL CORRUPTION SERIES
*Corrupt*
*Defile*
*Consume*
*Ravage*

## GIRL TALK SERIES:
*Seducing Lola*
*Tempting Sophia*
*Enticing Daphne*
*Charming Fiona*

## STANDALONE TITLES:
*One Knight Stand*
*Chance Encounters*
*Nightmares from Within*

## DEADLY LOVE SERIES:
*Destructive*
*Addictive*

# Chapter One

## Blythe

Standing in front of the historic red brick building felt like stepping back in time. It looked exactly the same as it had in my childhood. In fact, most of downtown Hope Valley looked just as it had when I used to live here. Sure, some of the shops and restaurants had changed names, and the building that once housed a title company was now a drycleaner, but other than that, it was as if not a day had passed since I'd last been there.

The glass on the massive windows was so clean it gleamed in the sunlight. The sign hanging above the door still had the familiar AO symbol in thick black letters, only it had clearly been touched up to keep it looking fresh.

Alpha Omega was owned and operated by a close

family friend, Lincoln Sheppard. Linc had always been such a great guy. I had enjoyed spending time with him and his family. His wife, Eden, was my mother's best friend, so we'd spent a ton of time together growing up. I hadn't spoken to either of them in a really long time and missed them both like crazy. I always thought I would enjoy reconnecting with them. I just never imagined it would be like *this*.

With a heavy sigh, I reached for the handle. My hand trembled as I pulled the heavy glass door open. Anxiety made my throat tight and my heart kick into high gear as I stepped inside the building. I couldn't believe this was happening, that I'd had to resort to *this*.

If you had asked me six months ago, I would have told you I was living my very best life. I had my kids, my dream house, and a husband I loved who, even though the honeymoon phase was long over, still doted on me. I was happy. *We* were happy. Or at least that's what I'd thought. I used to point out to Elliott how so many of the couples we'd been friends with had gone through contentious divorces and we were still going strong, and his response was always to kiss me and say, "It's easy to have a good marriage when you know how damn lucky you are." I'd always blushed at that, thankful that my husband could still make me swoon after three kids and nearly fifteen years of marriage.

Then, in the blink of an eye, that happiness was ripped away, and I'd been left questioning how much of what we had was real. I wasn't sure anything was worse than losing the man you loved, only to discover he wasn't the person you thought he was.

That was why I was here. I wanted answers. I *needed* them. Not knowing had eaten at me until I barely recognized the wilted, hollowed shell of a woman staring back at me when I looked in the mirror.

The girl behind the front desk looked up at the sound of the rubber soles of my shoes squeaking on the pristinely waxed tile floors. She smiled widely, her doe eyes growing even bigger as she greeted me. "Hi," she said cheerfully. "How can I help you?"

I could have gone to my stepfather, Trick, for help. He'd spent years working his way up through the police force before retiring a few years earlier. He still had all his connections, including his former partner and best friend, Hayes Walker, who was now the captain of the Hope Valley police department, and if there was anyone who could find the answers I was looking for, it was him. But the thought of having to peel off that particular Band-Aid to him and my mother was something I couldn't bear. I was heartbroken and angry and sad and betrayed. I couldn't handle feeling like a fool on top of everything else. And if I had to see the pity in their eyes when they discovered what I feared was the truth . . . well, I wasn't sure I could take that.

Trick was the closest thing anyone could wish to have as a father since he and my mom got together when I was just fourteen years old. He filled the gaping hole left behind by my biological father after he got tangled up with some really bad people. He'd gotten into drugs, selling and using, and that had resulted in my little brother and me being taken by the guy he'd screwed over. It had been one of the most terrifying events of my life, one that still gave me nightmares from time to time. Trick had been the one to save us. To love us. To heal us and help put us and our mother back together when it was all said and done.

The man loved me like I was his own flesh and blood, treating me the same as his own children, Hannah and Shawn, but I hadn't been able to bring myself to admit to my parents what had been weighing on me for the past few months, ever since Elliott died in that crash. This was something I needed to do on my own.

There was something about the receptionist I couldn't quite put my finger on. Something about her big eyes and bright smile rang familiar to me, but I wasn't sure why. I didn't realize I'd been staring until she cleared her throat and tried again, only this time more awkwardly. "Uh, hello. Do you need something?"

I blinked and gave my head a shake. "Yeah, sorry. It's just . . . you look—"

I was interrupted when a door to my left opened and a giant of a man stepped out. "Naomi, honey, you get that invoice for the Parker case scanned and emailed over?"

Suddenly I understood why the girl was so familiar.

I swallowed past the ball of cotton in my throat and attempted a smile in the direction of the man. His head was down, his eyes scanning the file he was holding, so he hadn't noticed me yet. "Hi, Linc."

His head shot up, vivid green eyes landing on me and widening as he slapped the folder shut and dropped his arms down to his sides.

"Well, I'll be." His mouth curved into a wide, bright grin that made my own just a little easier as he closed the distance between us and scooped me up, lifting my feet clear off the floor and squeezing tight enough that I could have sworn I heard my ribs crack. "If it isn't Little Blythe, all grown up."

I let out a wheezing chuckle and gave his back a pat before he returned me to the ground.

"No way!" The girl flew around the front desk fast as lightning, her arms replacing her father's in a hug much tighter than someone so tiny should have been capable of. "You're Blythe! It's been forever."

"I nodded, looking down at Lincoln and Eden's daughter. She'd barely been a toddler when I left for college at eighteen. Now she was all grown up, and absolutely *gorgeous*.

"It has. God, I can't believe you're an adult now. You look so much like your mom."

She smiled happily, taking that as the compliment it was meant to be.

I felt the squeeze of Lincoln's fingers around my forearm and then pressure as he gently guided me back around to face him.

The joy on his face quickly morphed into concern as he held me at arm's length and took me in. I knew I wasn't exactly at my best, but most days I had to put all my energy into piecing together some semblance of a life for my kids, who were still grieving the loss of their dad. Making sure they were okay took a lot of effort. What little I had left went into trying to lie in order to convince my loved ones I was all right. By that point, I was usually too drained to look after myself. I didn't know for sure if the clothes I'd put on that morning were clean or not. I just grabbed the first thing off the bedroom floor that didn't stink.

I was doing my best, but my best was sorely lacking, and on top of all that, I hated myself for failing my kids. I needed to do better for them. To *be* better. And the only way I could think to finally make that happen was to learn the truth. As long as these questions were plaguing me, I wouldn't be able to move on.

"We were all sorry to hear about Elliott, sweetheart."

I sniffled, willing the burn in my eyes to fade away. I was so tired of crying.

My voice came out in a croak as I spoke softly. "Thanks. I appreciate that."

"If there's anything we can do to help, don't hesitate to ask."

"Actually, that's why I'm here. I want to hire you to find some information for me."

His forehead creased as his brows pulled into a frown. "Blythe, honey, have you talked to your dad about this? Maybe he could help you—"

I shook my head, cutting him off with a desperate look. "I need to do it this way. I'll pay. It doesn't matter how much."

"Sweetheart, you don't have to—"

"Please, Lincoln." The pleading quality of those two whispered words brought the huge man up short. "Please. I just . . . I need to do it this way."

I could see the indecision warring on his face, and despite the time that had passed, I knew him well enough to know he was struggling between wanting to help me and concern he might somehow be stepping on

Trick's toes. If there was one thing I knew about Lincoln Sheppard that would *never* change, it was his loyalty.

My heart started to sink at the thought that he might turn me away. But after a handful of excruciating seconds, he let out a heavy sigh and said, "All right."

The relief I felt was so profound that my shoulders sagged forward, and it was a wonder my knees didn't give out from under me.

Lincoln looked in Naomi's direction, saying, "Can you call—?"

"Already on it," she assured him before he even finished his sentence, picking up the receiver on her desk and tapping against a few of the buttons.

"Come on, then," Linc said to me, stepping to the side and extending his arm, guiding me toward the office off to the left. "Let's talk in private."

My legs felt wooden and stiff as I crossed the threshold and moved to one of the two chairs in front of the large wooden desk. The door clicked shut behind me just before Lincoln rounded the desk and took a seat in the leather executive chair, bracing his elbows on the arms and steepling his fingers. "As soon as my partner gets here, we can start."

A flutter of panic filled my chest. "Partner?"

He leaned forward, his features growing tender. "It's

okay, Blythe. He knows the rules. Discretion is the name of the game."

I nodded, trying to ease my racing heart. I trusted Lincoln. If he said this guy was trustworthy, I believed it. "I didn't know you'd taken on a partner," I said, trying my hand at casual conversation.

Lincoln smiled warmly. "It's more of a mentorship and training deal than a partnership, really. Eden's been on my ass about retiring for a while now. She wants to travel, and I want to give her that. I brought him on so I could teach him to take over before eventually handing over the reins."

"Oh wow." That was huge, him teaching someone how to replace him. Alpha Omega was Lincoln's baby. He's built it from the ground up when he moved to Hope Valley after his time in the military. He'd hand-picked the entire crew, hiring mostly people who'd left the military behind and were looking for something to do with their lives. It could be hard to reacclimate to civilian life after serving your country for so many years, and Alpha Omega was a place where they could belong.

For Lincoln to hand over the keys to the castle like that, this guy had to be like family, and it spoke to how much he cherished his wife to say goodbye to everything he'd created just because she wanted him to. "That's huge."

He smiled again, nodding. "It is, but it's time. How about you tell me what brought you in while we're waiting. He won't have any problem catching up."

Okay. I could do this. I could say the words I'd yet to say out loud in the months that had passed since my husband died.

I pulled in a centering breath and opened my mouth. The words spilled out right as the door to the office swung open and the very last person I would ever want to confess my shame to stepped inside.

"I want you to find out how long my husband was cheating on me."

# Chapter Two



## Rhodes

I didn't know what I was stepping into when I grabbed the knob to Lincoln's office and twisted. All Naomi told me when she rang my office was that Lincoln needed me for a consultation.

This had been happening more often lately, ever since Linc decided he was going to step away from the business and wanted me to take over. Anytime a new case came in, he called me in on it, basically giving me lead to handle it the way I saw fit.

To say I'd been surprised when he told me he wanted to hand Alpha Omega over to me would have been a serious understatement. I'd wanted to work for the man for as long as I could remember. Lincoln Sheppard and the guys who worked for him were legends in our small town. They were so good at what they did that they were frequently hired by famous actors and actresses, singers, athletes, and millionaires all across the country.

I'd idolized the guys from Alpha Omega. To a kid like me—a kid who'd been forced to grow up on the wrong side of the tracks because our parents had taken off on us, leaving my older sister, Gypsy, to try and keep a roof over our heads—they were the closest thing to celebrities I thought I'd ever get a chance to see. Then everything changed when Marco came into our lives.

Marco Castillo wasn't only part of the Alpha Omega crew, he was also the closest thing to a father figure my younger siblings and I ever had. He'd fallen in love with Gypsy, and despite her baggage—five younger siblings you were responsible for raising was a *hell* of a lot of baggage—he'd held firm that she was the one for him. He never wavered, even when my stubborn sister did everything in her power to push him away. He took us all on, rounding out our family, and making us whole. He was the missing piece none of us knew we needed. With him in my life, the infatuation I'd had for being one of the Alpha Omega elite changed.

It became less about them as a whole and more about Marco. He became an inspiration to me. I wanted to prove I was nothing like the sperm and egg donors who had created me, but more than that, I wanted to be a man as good as he was, as kind and big-hearted.

That was why I'd followed in his footsteps, enlisting in the Army before I was even out of high school and taking off for basic right after graduation. When my time with them was done, I'd come back home and applied for a job with Lincoln. All these years later, I was still trying to emulate the man who meant so damn much to me, still holding out hope that someday I might stop doubting myself and start believing I was worthy of all the good things the people who loved me believed I deserved. I kept hoping I'd stop feeling like I was tainted because of whose blood coursed through my veins. But it still haunted me.

I'd done a ton of work on myself over the years. Between my time in the Army teaching me how to be a man and all the therapy I'd done at Gypsy's insistence once I got home, I'd gotten better. But no matter how many years passed since I'd last laid eyes on my parents, I still sometimes felt like I couldn't scrub their dirt off my skin. Some days I still saw myself as that boy who'd been ridiculed by his classmates for growing up poor and living in a piece-of-shit, run-down trailer.

Gypsy had done everything in her power to make sure we all had everything we needed growing up. Even going so far as dancing at a shithole strip club just to make sure there was enough money to feed us and keep a roof over our heads. Granted, it wasn't much of a roof, that was for damn sure, but at least we had *something*. There wasn't anything she wouldn't have done for every one of us, and any good that was inside me was solely because of her.

I owed her my life.

I didn't bother knocking since Linc and the potential client on the other side of the door were expecting me, but nothing could have prepared me for the woman sitting across from Lincoln.

"I want you to find out how long my husband was cheating on me."

*What the fuck?*

I came up short, jerking to a stop as the last word passed her lips.

She spun around in her chair, and that first glimpse of her face was an iron fist right to my solar plexus. I knew she was back in town. I'd known almost from the moment she crossed the town line. It was nearly impossible not to know something like that in a town this size, but even though I'd been waiting for this very moment for weeks—anticipating it, fucking *praying* for it—I was still caught off guard.

I'd dreamed of the moment I'd finally see Blythe again after all these years. Of what I'd say to her, how I'd apologize for ruining us. But all the words I'd memorized flew right out of my head at the sight of her.

"Rhodes."

My name came out of her mouth in a single breath. The sound of her saying my name used to slam right into my chest hard enough to send me flying backward, but I was too focused on what she looked like for my body to react as viscerally as it used to. Still, there was a flare behind my ribs at the sound of it.

"Blythe." I choked out her name, my voice a throaty rasp, as if I hadn't used it in far too long. My feet started moving without input from my brain. All these years later and the hold she had on me was still as strong. She pulled me in without having to try, her gaze alone like a tractor beam, reeling me in, and I was all too happy to let it lead me without any fight.

Her eyes were two pools of the most gorgeous blue I'd ever seen, and looking into them felt like diving right into the warm waters of the Caribbean. But those hypnotic eyes were the only thing about her that reminded me of the girl I'd once known.

Everything else about her had changed in a way that twisted my stomach into tangled knots. Her hair lacked the luster it used to have, lying flat on her head and hanging limp down around her shoulders. Her cheeks were sunken, and her clothes hung off of her like she'd lost weight she couldn't afford to lose. Her skin was unnaturally pale everywhere except the dark purple circles the color of bruises beneath her eyes.

She looked like she hadn't slept in weeks or eaten in just as long, and something acutely primal and deep inside me roared with the need to haul her into my arms and carry her the fuck out of there so I could take her somewhere safe and quiet to get the rest she so clearly needed. Every protective instinct I had was screaming to take all of her problems and carry them myself if it meant I could relieve her of the burden. I'd always had a strong protective instinct, but it had been out of control when it came to Blythe, and apparently, that hadn't changed.

It wasn't until I was standing two feet away that I recalled what she had been saying when I opened the door.

*"I want you to find out how long my husband was cheating on me."*

That one sentence shouldn't have had me seeing red, not when I hadn't seen this woman in damn near two decades, but a crimson haze was slowly spreading across my vision. "What happened? Are you okay?"

I knew in an instant I'd handled this all wrong. Her eyes widened, and I didn't miss the flash of panic that filled the turquoise depths. She looked cagier than a rabbit facing down a coyote, ready to take off at any moment.

"Um . . . I think maybe this was a mistake. I should go."

Lincoln held his hand up to stop her as she started to push up from the chair she was sitting in. "Please, just stay. And you"—he pointed at me, his face hard as he stared me down—"sit and calm the hell down."

I was a forty-two-year-old man who'd seen more than my fair share of shit in my lifetime, yet the man in front of me could still manage to make me feel like a goddamn kid with only a few words and that damn tone of his.

It blew my mind that a man who wielded that kind of power, the kind of power that could still cause the balls to draw up on every grown man he so much as glared threateningly at, was so tightly wound around his daughter's finger. I'd witnessed her laugh more than once when he tried using the same tone on her. She just giggled and patted his chest placatingly, like it was all some big joke. I had a feeling more than half of the gray hairs he sported weren't due to age as much as they were from her.

Clamping my mouth shut, I moved to the empty chair beside Blythe and slowly lowered down. The last thing I wanted was to spook her and send her running for the hills, but I couldn't bring myself to rip my gaze off her face. "Sorry," I muttered and pulled in a calming breath, trying to steady my racing heart.

Linc bobbed his head in a single nod before turning back to Blythe and smiling softly. "All right, sweetheart. There's no need for you to worry. Discretion is the name of the game here. You have my word. Anything you say in here stays between us. Rhodes and I won't tell a soul."

The muscle in her jaw ticked beneath her skin as she clenched her teeth. If I hadn't been watching her so closely, I might have missed the emotion that flashed across her face faster than a person could blink. But I had been watching, and I couldn't miss it. It also helped that I knew her as well as I did. It might have been nearly twenty years ago, but there was a time when she'd been the most important person in my life. She'd been my whole world.

The emotion was shame.

I hated seeing it on her beautiful face, and I swore to myself at that very moment I would do everything in my power to take her shame away.

# Chapter Three

Blythe

The mattress dipping a couple feet away yanked me awake in an instant. Such was the life of a mom. If it wasn't my internal clock waking me up with the sun, it was the faintest noise or slightest movement.

I knew what I would see even before I flipped my eyelids open, and sure enough, the instant my vision cleared, I found myself staring into the sleepy-eyed, pillow-creased face of my four-year-old daughter, Ainsley, lying on the pillow beside mine.

I curved my lips into a tired grin. "Morning, baby girl."

And just like I knew what I'd see as soon as I woke up, I also knew what was coming next.

"Mornin' Mommy." She smiled big, showcasing

every one of her tiny white baby teeth. "My tummy said it wants waffles."

*Called it.*

Of course it did. My little girl wanted waffles every morning. If she could, she would eat waffles for every single meal and never get tired of them.

I let out a low chuckle, the sound still raspy with sleep. "Your tummy said that, huh?"

Her head bobbed up and down as she blinked her big blue eyes at me. "Yuh-huh. It grumbled really loud. Like a monster."

"Let me guess. It said *feed me waffles?*" I asked, adopting a low, growly monster voice and lifting my hands in front of my face and curling my fingers so they looked like claws.

My baby let out a giggle that filled my chest with warmth. It was nice to feel it, especially since that warmth had been lacking in recent months. It was hard enough to mourn the loss of Elliott, but the rage at the realization that he had been cheating piled on top of all that sorrow. I bounced between crying because I missed him to wishing he was still alive so I could yell and cuss him out and slap him across the face for betraying our marriage. Trying to keep his memory alive for my kids, smiling as they remembered the happy times with their father, was a knife to my heart, over and over again. But I couldn't bring myself to tarnish him in their eyes. As far as I was concerned, they never needed to know.

I'd been keeping Elliott's secrets to myself for months and they were starting to eat at my insides. It had gotten so bad it had driven me to Alpha Omega and to a blast from my past I hadn't been prepared for.

I hadn't been thrilled to reveal all my secrets to Rhodes, the first boy to break my heart—confessing that the last man I'd been with had shattered it all over again —but the need for answers kept me from bolting out of there.

To my surprise, by the time I finished telling Linc and Rhodes my story, I'd left their office feeling a bit lighter. It was nice no longer being the only one to carry the weight of my deceased husband's infidelity.

I pushed up to sitting, shoving the tangled mop of my hair out my face. "Are you sure the monster in your belly didn't say it wanted oatmeal?"

Her face pinched up like I'd just suggested we eat dog poo for breakfast. "No, Mommy," she said with more seriousness than a little four-year-old should have been capable of. "It said waffles. I heard it." Her Rs still came out sounding like Ws, making her solemnity that much more adorable.

Throwing the covers back, I climbed out of the bed and lifted my arms high, stretching the last of the sleep from my body. "Okay, chickadee. Let's go see about taking care of that monster, huh?"

"Yay!" She sprang to her feet on my bed and hopped her way to the foot before launching herself off, barely giving me a second to brace to catch her. I let out an *oof* as I got my arms around her just in time. She'd hit another growth spurt recently—it seemed like she was hitting one every other week—and it was getting harder and harder to hold my baby girl. It was only a matter of time before she would be too heavy for me to hold, and I didn't think there was anything I could do to prepare for that.

I propped her on my hip and brushed her fiery red mass of curls out of her face to press a kiss to her temple. That hair was something she'd gotten from my mother, along with her sassy personality. She also shared the same shade of turquois blue eyes as my mother and me. She looked like a miniature version of Nona Wanderly while my other daughter Adeline and my son, Avett, both had their father's chestnut hair and velvety umber eyes.

I'd always loved that two of my babies shared their dad's goldish brown eyes, but now every time I had a thought like that, a sour taste formed in my mouth and my stomach twisted up. I hated that all my happy thoughts of my husband felt tainted now. I could only hope that the pain would eventually fade and I'd be able to look back at those memories without feeling like I'd been kicked in the chest with a steel-toed boot. But for now, I'd continue to pretend for the sake of my kids.

I descended the stairs to the first floor with Ainsley still attached to my hip and headed for the kitchen, successfully skirting the gigantic running shoes scattered about and stepping over the dirty socks on the living room floor. We'd been crashing with my brother Tristan since moving back to Hope Valley, and he wasn't the best at housekeeping. Fortunately, I was a pro at dodging all sorts of tripping hazards thanks to three kids who weren't big on putting their stuff away. The only thing I couldn't seem to avoid were Legos. Those tiny little bastards were created by Satan to torture parents. I was convinced they contained black magic and appeared out of thin air the second before you stepped down.

Tristan's dog, Doc—named after his favorite movie character, Doc Holliday—lifted his head from his dog bed in the corner of the living room and gave me a tired blink before standing on his stumpy legs and stretching his oddly shaped body.

He was part pit bull and part English bulldog, the combination creating something . . . unique. Tristan had gotten him in the hopes of teaching him to be a guard dog, but the joke was on my little brother.

Doc looked like he should be ferocious, with his short, pointed ears, strong face, and stocky body, but he was an equal combination of lazy and pathetic that basically made him useless for anything other than cuddling. I hadn't known it was possible for a dog to be so damn whiny. God forbid he stepped on something sharp or another dog barked at him. There was even one time when a bird swooped down in an effort to peck him. It didn't, of course, but it got close. Doc made a sound like he was dying and collapsed on the ground, howling in agony until Tristan finally had to pick his heavy ass up.

He was utterly ridiculous and I loved him like crazy.

"Come on, Doc. Time to go potty." He stared at me for a few seconds, blinking as if to say *it's too damn early, woman* before finally giving in and slowly meandering behind me and Ainsley toward the kitchen.

I plopped my girl down on one of the barstools at the island with some paper and a few crayons, undid the latch that locked the doggy door in the back door so Doc could do his business, then got to work on breakfast.

Avett and Adeline were old enough now to appreciate sleeping in on weekends, so it was just me, my girl, and Doc as I cooked up a breakfast fit for a king. The only sounds in the sleepy house were the crackle of the bacon on the stove, the wheezy snores coming from where Doc was curled up in his kitchen dog bed—

because the spoiled K-9 was too delicate to lie on the bare floors, there was a fluffy dog bed in every room of the house—and the occasional chatter from Ainsley. Her favorite pastime was peppering people with ridiculous questions such as: *If you were a dragon what would be your favorite: spittin' fire or flyin'?* or *Why don't dogs go potty in boxes like cats?* or *Are Avett's farts so stinky 'cause his guts are rotten?*

That last one was a scientific anomaly, and I couldn't blame her for her curiosity. My son could clear a room in a matter of seconds.

Eventually, the cozy little bubble was broken when my brother came waltzing through the front door. He'd taken after our stepdad, Trick, and was a detective with the local police department. He'd been working odd hours lately because of a case, so it wasn't unusual for him to crash at the station for a few hours instead of coming home. At the sound of his daddy's key scraping into the deadbolt, Doc had burst out of the kitchen to greet him.

"Smells great in here," Tristan called through the living room seconds before he appeared in the kitchen, cradling his dog in his arms like a baby. Only his baby's legs were pointed straight in the air since they were too stubby for him to bend, and Doc's head hung backward over Tristan's bicep.

"Uncle Tris!" Ainsley shouted excitedly at the sight of my brother. With her level of enthusiasm, you would have thought Ains hadn't seen her uncle at lunch the day before, but I had a feeling that was due to them not getting to spend much time with him until recently.

I loved that they were so excited to be close to their uncle and Nana and Pop-Pop, but that also came with a heaping dose of guilt at the knowledge that they'd only just gotten close to my side of the family because of my own issues.

I'd had my reasons for wanting to escape Hope Valley when I was younger, and they were good enough reasons, but I never should have stayed away as long as I had. This wasn't a bad place, it just held unpleasant memories for me, so when Elliott and I were deciding where we wanted to start our life together after I graduated from college, I'd been all too agreeable when he suggested we move back to his hometown in Indiana.

My family had made the trek to see us countless times over the years, but I'd never returned the favor, and it took coming back here after Elliott died to realize how unfair I had been.

Tristan managed to put Doc down just in time to catch Ainsley as she Superman-ed off the barstool.

"Hey, squirt. What are you up to?"

"Me and Momma are makin' waffles," she announced proudly. "To feed the monster in my belly."

Tristan's eyes scanned the kitchen, growing wide before they landed on me. "Jesus, sis. You plannin' on feeding the entire neighborhood or something?"

I followed his line of sight, taking in the stack of fluffy Belgian waffles at least a foot and a half high, along with an entire package of bacon that I'd fried up, two different kinds of sausage—link and patty, because my children were picky eaters, even when it came to the shape of their food—scrambled eggs, home fries, and whipped cream I'd made from scratch.

Okay, so I might have gone a little overboard.

I waved him off, "It'll be fine. You'll eat at least half of this, and ever since Avett turned eight, it's like one of his legs hollowed out. What doesn't get eaten, I'll freeze for later."

My brother's brows lifted high on his forehead as he set Ainsley on the ground. "Squirt, why don't you and Doc go watch that annoying cartoon you love so much with those dogs shaped like rectangles."

Ainsley scowled up at Tristan with a murderous look on her face. "*Bluey* is *not* annoying!" she declared offendedly.

"My bad, baby girl." He placed his hands on her shoulders and spun her in the direction of the living room. "I'll give you five bucks to go watch it without arguing."

That was all it took for my girl to forget her uncle had just pissed her off. She skipped out of the kitchen, calling for Doc to follow her, and a minute later, the strains of the opening credits to her favorite show carried into the kitchen. Who knew a four-year-old could grasp the concept of a smart TV and its remote better than I could?

I turned my back on Tristan, picking up a dish towel to wipe down the counters that were crumb free and spotless, just so I had something to occupy myself and didn't have to see the apprehension on his face. I had a sneaking suspicion why he wanted privacy, and that suspicion was confirmed when he finally spoke.

"You're stress cooking."

*Damn it.*

Most people could hide their emotions easily enough, but I'd been cursed with an annoyingly obvious tell I'd gotten from my mom. Nona was a stress baker, had been for as long as I could remember. And while I didn't have her gift with pastries and sweets, I was a damn good cook. Unfortunately, when I was carrying a lot of anxiety, the only way for me to burn it off was to cook it out.

"I'm not stress cooking," I lied, though I knew it was

pointless. "It's just that Ainsley wanted waffles, and it's a huge pain in the ass to get the waffle maker out, so I made enough to freeze so the next time she asks, I can just pop them in the toaster."

He looked at me exasperatedly. "B, between the lasagnas, the chicken pot pie, the tomato bisque, the white bean chili, and the *seven* different types of bread you made from scratch, you can't possibly get anything else in that freezer."

Since the kids and I had moved in, I'd stress cooked to the point that Tristan's freezer was so packed with soups and casseroles I'd run out of room and had to start stashing leftovers in my mom and Trick's freezer.

I shot him a glare over my shoulder. "It's not seven loaves of bread. You're exaggerating."

He let out a chortle. "I'm not. I actually counted. It's seven. Would have been eight, but I went overboard on that rosemary focaccia. You keep this shit up and I'm gonna have to buy a deep freezer to keep in the garage."

I gave him a look and tried for that mother guilt our mom had perfected and I'd been trying on my own kids more recently. "Well excuse me for trying to take care of the people I love."

The face he made told me my attempt failed. "Oh please!" He let out a scoffing laugh. "You can't guilt me. Maybe that would work if you were *our* mother, not the brat who shaved off the inner half of my eyebrows my sophomore year of high school."

I curled my lips between my teeth to keep from laughing and ended up making a sound like a choked snort. "You deserved it," I said, still refusing to apologize all these years later.

His jaw hinged open in affront. "It was the night before yearbook photos! I still get triggered to this day if someone pulls out that yearbook. I looked deranged, for Christ's sake."

A giggle forced its way past my lips. "That was payback for the Toby McGinnis debacle."

He threw his arms up in defense. "I was trying to help you out! He wanted to know if I thought he should ask you to the Homecoming dance, and I thought I was doing you both a favor by telling him to wait a week because you had PMS and were moody as hell."

I shot him a blank look. "You told him I had *HPV*, you dill hole."

"You know I got confused by all those acronyms. And don't act like I wasn't doing you a favor. You couldn't stand Toby, and there was no way in hell you wanted to go to the dance with him." He held his hands up in a stop motion and gave his head a shake. "Wait . . . I'm not having this argument again. You're just trying to change the subject from the fact that you're stressing out major about something."

"I'm not—"

The face he made cut my denial short. Gone was the little brother who I might have enjoyed tormenting as a kid, and in his place was a cop who wasn't in the mood to take any shit.

"Don't bother lying. I already know you're keeping something from me because more than one person told me they saw you walking into Alpha Omega yesterday."

*Son of a bitch.* I should have known it was only a matter of time until that juicy tidbit got out. I'd been gone too long and forgot that there really weren't any secrets in a small town.

The look on Tristan's face was a mixture of concern and hurt, and maybe a little disappointment. "I haven't pushed because I knew you were going through some tough shit, but you've been here for months, Blythe. It's time for you to tell me what's going on."

As I looked up into my little brother's eyes, a wave of guilt crashed over me. He was right. It was time I told him the truth.

# Chapter Four

## Blythe

I decided the best approach was to treat it as though I was ripping off a Band-Aid. Just spit it out and get it over with.

"Elliott was having an affair."

Tristan had been in the process of pouring himself a cup of coffee and jerked in shock at my announcement, sloshing the piping hot liquid over the lip of the mug and onto his hand.

"Shit!" He set the mug down with a *thunk* and shook the scalding liquid off his hand, a string of colorful curses streaming past his lips as I wet a rag at the sink.

"Christ, B. Warn a guy, why don't you?"

"Sorry," I said sheepishly as I took his hand and placed the cold, damp cloth on his red skin. "I didn't think you'd have that big a reaction. You okay?"

He took the rag from me and wrapped it around his fist. "It's fine. I've had worse. And you didn't think I'd have a big reaction to the fact my sister's husband—the father of my nieces and nephew—was screwing around on her?"

I heaved out a sigh, my shoulders dipping. It felt like all I was doing lately was sighing and slumping my shoulders in defeat. If I wasn't careful, I was going to screw up my posture permanently. I moved to the barstool Ainsley had vacated and collapsed onto it, bracing my elbows on the counter and scrubbing at my face with my hands.

"B?" Tristan asked, concern laced through his tone.

I looked up just as he rounded the island to take the stool beside mine. He held his cup of coffee in one hand and slid another cup in front of me, doctored up just the way I liked it based on the rich toffee color of the liquid.

"You already know he wasn't alone in the car the night of the crash."

Tristan nodded his head. It had been a tragedy that had taken two lives. My husband's and the life of the woman in the passenger seat beside him.

"He told me he was going out of town for a conference, so I'd assumed she was a colleague from the university. Another professor in his department or something."

He drank from his cup, his eyes riveted to the side

of my face as I stared into my own, twirling it around on the counter. "I'm guessing she didn't work with him?"

I gave my head a shake. "I found out during the wake." I could still remember the confusion on Bryan's face, the head of Elliott's department, when I'd mentioned the conference. How he shook his head, his eyes full of pity as he reached out to take my hand and tell me I must have been confused, there was no conference, and Elliott had put in for PTO the week he'd been out of town. I still remembered the condescending pat he'd given my hand, like I was just a bereaved widow whose imagination was running away from her before moving on to offer his condolences to Elliott's mother and father.

I'd walked around in a daze after that, my mind spinning out of control. I barely remembered anything that happened after that, running on autopilot as I tried to wrap my mind around what I heard. I was such a mess that it had taken two days for what Bryan said to fully sink in.

If he hadn't been at a literary conference, why had he been out of town? If the woman in the car with him wasn't a work colleague, who the hell was she?

"Once I was of sound enough mind to piece together the questions I needed to be asking, I went to Elliott's best friend. As soon as I asked if he knew why Elliott had been out of town, he got cagey."

Tristan's brows dipped together, his focus scrutinizing.

"He told me he didn't know, but I could tell he was lying. When I asked him about the woman, he said I just needed to leave it in the past. That digging things up wouldn't make me feel any better."

"Chickenshit," Tristan muttered.

I took a sip of my coffee. "That was basically my thought. I spent the next two months trying to get answers from Elliott's friends and family. Two months where everyone lied to my face or told me to let it go." I reached up to rub at the space between my brows, trying to ward off the headache I could feel building. That was only the second time I'd relayed the story, and already I was drained. Emotionally and physically. "I was grieving my husband, and at the same time, I'd never felt more alone. I felt like I was losing my mind, Tris. My husband had been lying to me, and not a single soul was willing to tell me the truth." I sniffled, blinking to fight back the burn of tears threatening to form. Those months in Indiana after Elliott's death had been the most isolating, heart-wrenching time in my life.

"I didn't have anyone," I admitted on a whisper. "The people I thought were my friends were more concerned about preserving a dead man's memory than giving me the answers I needed. I'd always thought of his parents as my second parents, but during those months it became clear I'd been so wrong." I looked at my brother, his face growing blurry as my eyes watered. "Do you have any idea what it feels like to have every single person in your life turn their back on you at the same time you discovered the person you loved—that you'd built a life with—had betrayed you?" As soon as the last word fell free, I lost the battle with my tears. "That's why I moved back here. I couldn't stay there. I was so alone, Tristan. And everywhere I turned, there were memories of Elliott."

"Christ, B." He leaned forward, his long arms circling around me and pulling, forcing me and the stool closer so he could wrap me in a tight embrace. "I'm so damn sorry." I sniffled again, sinking deeper into his embrace and accepting the comfort he was offering. For the first time in a really long time, I was starting to feel like I wasn't completely alone. "I fuckin' hate that you were dealing with that by yourself. I wish I could have been there for you."

I gave him a squeeze. "You're helping now. You've been helping since I moved back."

We separated and Tristan raked a hand through his

hair in frustration as he lifted his mug for another drink. "How did you finally find out?"

I gripped my own cup, hoping the warmth of the ceramic would seep through my palms and warm me from the inside. "I was packing up his office and found some pictures he'd stuffed in the back of his desk drawer."

I'd barely managed to make it to the bathroom in time to lose the very limited contents of my stomach after seeing those pictures, and once I'd gotten ahold of myself, I'd taken them into the kitchen and set them on fire, dropping them into the sink and watching the edges burn as the images of the couple in them distorted and burned up.

"That motherfucker," Tristan hissed. "That stupid son of a bitch. I want to bring him back to life just so I can kill him all over again."

That burn returned to my eyes at the conviction in my brother's voice. Leaning to the side, I rested my head against his shoulder, grateful that he cared so damn much.

"I guess this is how Alpha Omega came into play? You asked them to dig into their relationship?"

I nodded, not missing the disappointment in his tone at the thought that I went to someone other than him to help me.

"Does Mom know?" he asked after several seconds of silence.

I shook my head, unable to find the words.

"Dad?" he asked, meaning Trick.

I let out another shake.

"Christ, B. Why didn't you tell me? Why didn't you tell *any of us*? We could have helped you. Or at the very least, been there for you."

I sat up straight, that shame coming back with a vengeance. "I didn't tell anybody, Tris. I was humiliated."

His head whipped around, his gaze fierce. "*What?*"

"I was embarrassed." The tears started falling faster, making tracks down my cheeks and falling onto the counter in tiny little splashes. "I swore to myself that I would never *ever* fall for a man like our biological father, and look what I did." I threw my hands up in the air. "I married a cheater and a liar, and I was completely blind to it. I couldn't ask you or Dad to help because I couldn't stand the thought of telling you all of this. My whole marriage was a lie. I'm a giant failure."

"Oh, Blythe." His eyes grew soft and sad as he twisted all the way around on the stool to face me full on. "B, you aren't a failure. Elliott was the failure. *He* failed to live up to his vows. *He* failed to be the husband you deserved. *He* failed to be the kind of man who deserves you. But don't get things twisted. He's nothing like the piece of shit who spawned us. Elliott was piece of shit, but our bio dad was a goddamn psychopath. You didn't marry him. You married a flawed human being."

I wiped at my cheeks and let out a shuttered breath. "I'm just so *mad*," I admitted quietly, my voice vibrating with all the built-up pain and anger I'd been holding on to for months. "My insides feel like a soda that's been shaken up and is about to explode, but I have nowhere to point all these feelings. I want to scream at him . . . but he's gone, and it's not fair."

"Then scream."

I looked at my brother with a frown. "What?"

"You want to scream, then scream. You can't do it at him, but there's no reason you have to keep it all inside. You want to rage and hit something, do it. I've got a heavy bag hangin' in the garage you can wail on as long as you want. Hell, I'll give you a baseball bat and one of the piece-of-shit fax machines from the station and let you go all *Office Space* on it. You want to cry or cuss, do it. Just stop holding it in, B. It's eating away at you, and I hate that it's making my fierce, vibrant, ball-bustin' sister fade away."

I swiped at my nose with the back of my hand and let out a watery laugh. "When did you become a grownup?" I teased.

He shot me a cocky grin and buffed his nails on the shoulder of his shirt. "I have my moments."

"I see that." I released a slow, steady breath, feeling some of the weight lift away that had been sitting on my chest for the past several months. "Thank you, Tris."

His arm came around my shoulders, and he pulled me into his side. "Always, B. Don't ever forget that. I will *always* be here for you."

He couldn't possibly know how much that meant to me.

# Chapter Five

## Rhodes

I'd been at my computer for so long the information on the screen was starting to blur. The blue light was giving me a headache that was steadily building into a migraine, but I couldn't make myself look away. I kept hoping what I was looking at was wrong, that I'd stumbled across incorrect information, but I knew that wasn't the case. It wasn't my ego talking when I claimed I was good at my job. It was the truth.

There was a reason Lincoln had chosen me to take over when he retired, and it wasn't the family connections. Well, not *just* the family connections. He and Marco were still tight, and his wife Eden was part of my sister Gypsy's crew of besties—had been since I was back in high school.

They were family by choice, not blood, but family all the same.

"You look like you're contemplatin' pickin' up that monitor and chuckin' it out the window."

I cast a quick look to my opened office door to find Linc standing in the doorway. Leaning back in my chair, I pushed out a heavy breath and pinched the bridge of my nose. "You aren't too far off the mark."

My boss and mentor moved into my office and, taking one of the chairs across from me, kicked his feet up on the edge of my desk, making himself comfortable. "Three guesses as to what's got you lookin' like you're ready to commit murder, and I don't need the second two."

I remained silent, knowing I didn't need to speak to prompt him to continue. Sure enough, he spoke a second later. "This have to do with the case your girl brought us?"

My chest tightened like my ribs were doing their best to squeeze the air from my lungs. "She's not my girl," I said in a low rumble.

Lincoln arched a brow at me. "Could've fooled me, the way you acted when you first laid eyes on her. Thought I was gonna have to lock you down to keep you from doin' somethin' stupid."

I shot him a bored look. "Did you forget why she came in here in the first place?" Because I sure as hell hadn't. "She's been off living her own life for years now."

"And you've been sitting here stagnant that whole damn time."

I jerked back in my chair at his declaration. My lips parted, but I couldn't seem to form any words.

"Don't think I haven't noticed, son. That we haven't *all* noticed."

My throat grew uncomfortably tight, causing my words to come out in a rasp as I said, "I don't know what you're talking about."

"I'm talkin' about the fact that there hasn't been a single woman who's played a significant role in your life since you took off for the Army when you were eighteen. I'm talkin' about the fact that you've spent the past several years goin' through women like most people go through underwear, and you never once got close to settlin' down."

"That's not true," I argued. "I've had relationships."

Linc's mouth flattened into a thin line. "And did a single one of those relationships have any substance to them? Did you ever really let any of them in?" He lifted a single brow. "Did you ever introduce any of them to your family?"

I clamped down on the inside of my cheek to keep from telling him to fuck off. This was a man I respected the hell out of, but just then, I was pissed as hell that he'd managed to read me so damn well.

I also hated that what he said made me feel like a dick. I didn't want to be that asshole when it came to women, but what he said was the truth. I'd made a few attempts at something real and lasting over the years, but no matter how hard I tried, I always seemed to have one foot out the door.

The last woman I'd seen exclusively lasted a little over six months, and that had been the longest relationship I'd had since Blythe. I'd been happy enough and was content to keep things going. Until Grace started talking about the future. She'd casually started asking if I thought I might want kids some day and if I saw myself getting married, and more than once she mentioned coming along with me to the family dinners I had with my siblings once a week. I'd hated hurting her, but I couldn't see any of those things with her, so I ended it.

The breakup had been painful on both sides, but necessary. She was a good woman and she deserved a man who could give her what she wanted. That man wasn't me.

"I don't know why we're even talking about this.

Blythe and I ended more than twenty years ago. We were just kids back then, for Christ's sake."

Lincoln crossed his thick arms over his barrel chest. The man might have been well past middle age, but damn if he looked it. "So were Tempie and Hayes when they first found each other," he reminded me, speaking of two more close friends tied to Gypsy's inner circle. "If you recall, they'd been split for nearly as long as you and Blythe. And look what happened there."

The parallels between my relationship with Blythe and the police captain's marriage were uncanny. They'd also been high school sweethearts. They'd also broken up and gone their separate ways—Tempie to Chicago and Hayes to the Marines. Tempie had come back when the aunt who raised her passed away, and the two of them discovered they'd never stopped loving each other. They were still happily married to this day.

"Blythe and I aren't Tempie and Hayes," I grumbled. The distinct difference between us and them was the fact that neither of them had moved on during their time apart. They hadn't married or had kids.

Lincoln held up his hands in surrender. "Okay, if you say so. I'll let it go."

"Appreciate it."

"Just answer one question and I'll never bring it up again."

"Christ," I grunted. The throb that had been building behind my eyes suddenly doubled in intensity. "What is it?"

"In all your diggin' into their background, can you say with certainty that the man she was married to and had kids with truly deserved her?"

*Fuck me.* I couldn't say a word. He had me, and judging from the slow, knowing smile that tilted the corners of his mouth, the fucker knew it too.

"Thought so." He pushed up on the arms of the chair and rose to his considerable height. "So are you gonna be the one to tell her that piece of shit had a whole other family on the side, or do you want me to do it?"

I threw my hands up in the air in exasperation. I should have known he'd pull some shit like that. "Jesus, Linc. If you're just gonna run your own investigation every damn time, why bother having me do it as well?"

He shrugged his wide shoulders unapologetically. "What can I say? I was curious and got a bit snoopy."

That seemed to be the case more often than not. The guy was a nosy pain in the ass. But his question brought my back up straight. "I don't think I should be the one to give her the truth," I confessed. It had been obvious the moment I'd walked into Lincoln's office that she hadn't wanted me there, and she'd been hesitant to give me the story. There would be no comfort for her when she found out the whole truth—that it hadn't just been an affair—and my gut told me that I was the last person she'd want to hear it from.

Lincoln nodded gravely. "I understand. I'll take care of it."

My ribs squeezed the hell out of my lungs again when I thought about how she'd take the news, and I would have given my own life to be able to comfort her when the time came. Unfortunately, I'd lost that right a long time ago.

I PULLED my truck to a stop in front of the big red-brick house on Magnolia drive and threw it into park, hitting the button to kill the ignition. The house that Marco had bought for Gypsy and the rest of us years ago was still the central hub for all family gatherings, which worked fine for me. I loved my family with everything in me, but when I purchased my house years back, I'd done it for the solitude and the quiet. I'd made sure it was big enough to house the entire Bradbury-Castillo clan if necessary, but I wasn't really a fan of playing host, so as long as my oldest sister was game, I'd let her. I was more than happy to show up, eat, catch up with my crazy family, then head home when the noise and chaos got to be too much.

I pushed the front door open and was immediately greeted with the sounds of laughter and conversation coming from the kitchen at the back of the house. "I'm here," I called out, and my words were met with the almost immediate pounding of tiny feet on the hard-wood floors. I managed to brace just in time for a tornado of dark hair and an overabundance of energy to slam into my thighs.

My nephew, Cooper, looked up at me with a huge grin, a hole where his left lateral incisor had been the last time I saw him. "Uncle Rhodes!"

After raising the five of us, Gypsy and Marco had decided not to have kids of their own, saying we were all they needed, but now that we were grown, there was no limit to the amount of guilt my big sister was willing to lay on each of us to see to it that we started popping out kiddos of our own. So far, my sister Sunny was the only one to give her what she so desperately wanted.

Sunny and her husband, Aaron, had two kids: twelve-:year-old Brynne and seven-year-old Cooper. The rest of us had made it our mission to spoil them rotten.

I rustled the hair on the top of his head and returned his infectious smile. "Hey, bub. How you doin'?"

"Good! Can I go for a ride on your motorcycle?"

I let out a chuckle. It was the same question he asked every time he saw me, so I followed it up with the same question I always asked in return. "What'd your mom say?"

He bit down on his bottom lip and cast his eyes to the left in an obvious effort to think up a lie. "She said sure!"

"Uh-huh," I returned skeptically just as the sister in question stepped into the entryway.

"I said over my cold, dead body, mister. And if you keep going around telling stories, you're gonna lose iPad privileges."

Cooper hit me with a sheepish smile before the expression on his face drooped into what could only be described as hangdog and turned to his mother. He'd even managed to perfect poking his bottom lip out and everything. "Sorry, Momma," the little actor offered remorsefully.

Sunny rolled her eyes, but I didn't miss the tension around her mouth as she tried to fight back a laugh. "Sure you are. Go help Auntie Holly and Uncle Lee set the table."

My nephew bolted off toward the kitchen, and I

moved to Sunny, bending to press a kiss to her cheek. "Hey, Sun. How you doin'?"

She wrapped her arms around my middle and gave me a quick squeeze before sliding herself beneath my arm so it was draped over her shoulders as she guided me toward the noises coming from the back of the house. "I'm good. Tired—as usual. Between Coop trying in every way known to man to break every bone in his body and Brynne morphing into an angsty pre-teen, it's a wonder I haven't pulled all my hair out."

I gave her a squeeze and let out another laugh just as we hit the open concept kitchen and dining area.

"I remember when you were an angsty pre-teen," Gypsy said as she moved around the massive island in our direction. "Hey, honey." She lifted up on her toes to kiss my cheek, and I dropped my hold on Sunny in order to embrace my oldest sister and lift her feet off the ground. She might not have been the one to bring us into the world, but she'd been the closest thing the five of us ever had to a mother, so I gave her the respect and devotion usually assigned to the role.

"Hey, back. Dinner smells fantastic."

"It's Detty's Fettucine Alfredo," she said in return.

Growing up in the trailer park, there had been an older woman who helped Gypsy take care of us. Odette, or Detty, as we'd called her, wasn't blood, but she was more family than our own parents, and was a surrogate grandmother to all six of us Bradbury kids. We were so close with her that when Marco had bought this house, he'd chosen it because of the in-law suite in the back so Detty could leave the trailer park with us.

Gypsy had been decent enough of a cook, but once we moved in here and there was more room, Detty had decided to teach Gypsy everything she knew, and my sister had gone from good to great. We lost Detty about fourteen years ago, but her memory still lived on in so many ways, including the recipes she'd passed down to my sister.

Detty's Fettucine Alfredo was one of my favorites.

I moved around the kitchen, greeting the rest of my family and ending at Marco, who clasped my hand and jerked me in for a quick, backslapping hug before pulling back and studying my face closely. "You good?"

My brow furrowed in confusion. I noticed everyone was watching me more intently than was normal. "Yeah, I'm great."

Sunny's brows climbed high on her forehead. "You sure?"

"Uh . . . what's goin' on guys?"

Holly, my youngest sister and the most emotional one out of the whole crew rushed me and wrapped me in a hug so tight my ribs protested. "We know about Blythe coming into your office yesterday."

*Fucking small towns.*

"Jesus," I grunted. *Not this shit again,* I thought as I worked to extricate myself from my tiny sister's iron hold. "It's all good. You guys don't need to hover like this. I'm fine. Really."

Raylan sauntered up, all cowboy swagger is his Wranglers and dusty boots. He handed me a non-alcoholic beer that Gypsy kept stocked in her fridge just for me and clapped me on the shoulder. "Not hoverin', just concerned. We know seein' her again couldn't have been easy."

"It's not like we don't know you're still in love with her," my youngest brother, Raleigh—Lee for short— chimed in.

Sunny looked at me, her eyes glowing with sympathy. "She's my best friend, and you're my brother. It still kills me that you guys didn't work out."

I wasn't sure how much more of this I could take. I'd gone twenty years without much mention of Blythe from my family, but now that she was back, it was like the floodgates had opened. Lifting the beer to my lips, I drained more than half in a couple large gulps, wishing it was something stronger. There weren't many times in my life that I'd wished for a drink, but on the rare occurrence, I simply had to remind myself why I'd made the conscious decision years ago not to touch the stuff. Our folks weren't *just* neglectful. They were drunks as well, so I made sure I'd never go down that road, because I didn't want to be anything like them.

"Look, I appreciate you guys caring, but if it's all the same, I'd rather change the subject."

"We can do that," Gypsy said, using a tone that brooked no argument. "Dinner's ready anyway, so let's eat."

The rest of the evening went off without a hitch. Despite the ache in my chest that I hadn't been able to shake since laying eyes on Blythe in Lincoln's office yesterday, I'd managed to enjoy my time with my family. I even laughed at my nephew's crazy antics.

By the time I said my goodbyes and headed for my truck, I was beyond tired and looking forward to face-planting in my bed and not moving until morning.

"Rhodes, wait."

I let out a sigh at the sound of Sunny's voice and stopped halfway down the walkway to turn and face her as she pulled the front door closed and made her way to me, worry creasing her forehead.

She pulled her cardigan tight around herself and crossed her arms over her chest as she stopped in front of me. "What did Blythe want?"

My features went soft. "You know I can't talk to you about that, Sun," I said gently.

She lowered her head on a sigh and gave it a dejected shake before her glassy eyes came back to mine. "I know. I'm sorry for asking. I don't want to put you in a tough spot. I just . . . I'm worried about her. She hasn't been the same since she came back, and I don't think it's only about losing Elliott." I might not have had the right to talk to Blythe over the past two decades, but she and Sunny never stopped being best friends, even from separate states.

She paused, pulling the corner of her lip between her teeth and biting down. "Can you at least tell me if she's okay?"

I reached out, and gave her bicep a squeeze. "That's not for me to say. Just keep doing what you're doing. Keep showin' her you care. As long as she's got good people lookin' out for her, she'll get through this."

Sunny's head canted to the side, her gaze scrutinizing. "You really do still love her, don't you?"

There was no point in lying. "I do," I said, the confession like a knife to the heart. "I never stopped."

The sympathy in my sister's eyes nearly killed me. "Then maybe this is your second chance. Whatever she's going through, maybe you're the one who's supposed to help her through to the other side." I opened my mouth to argue, but she reached up and cupped my cheek, silencing me. "I've always believed in fate, Rhodes, and I believe there's a reason you could never bring yourself to settle down."

With that, she turned on her heel and skip-walked back into Gypsy's house, leaving me to try to stuff down the little pang of hope that her words gave root to.

# Chapter Six

## Blythe

I let out a yawn and sucked back the remaining dregs in my coffee mug before refocusing on the invoice on the computer screen in front of me. I'd never been a fan of clerical work, but when I got to Hope Valley I hadn't really been in a position to be picky when it came to finding a job. Unlike Elliott, I hadn't had a clear idea of what I wanted to do once I graduated from college. He'd known he wanted to teach—hell, we met because he was TAing one of my classes. I'd gotten a degree in business management mainly because it sounded good, but I spent the first few years of our marriage bouncing from job to job, trying to find my passion. I eventually discovered it when Avett came along. I loved being a stay-at-home mother, but without

Elliott's paycheck, I'd needed to find a source of income fast.

Sure, there was Social Security, and Elliott and I both had life insurance policies, but I would have rather put that money away for my kids' future than live off of it, so not long after returning to my hometown, I'd started my job hunt. None of the jobs I'd applied for filled me with excitement, but I told myself it was about taking care of my family, not finding the perfect fit. I applied for anything I thought I might have been reasonably qualified for, and the first callback was for a receptionist/file clerk for a local OBGYN and reproductive endocrinologist. The work could be mind-numbing, but Dr. Shaundry was kind, the pay was good, and the other women on staff were easy to work with. It could have been worse.

"So, I told him if he wanted *that* in the bedroom, he'd have to do better than an all-you-can-eat pizza buffet and a pitcher of beer at the bowling alley," our lab tech, Diana, continued, recounting her latest dating fiasco to our office manager, Gretchen. "For that, I expected a lobster dinner with a side of filet mignon."

Gretchen let out a whoop of laughter. "And what did he have to say about that?"

Diana scoffed. "That he wasn't gonna shell out that kind of money until he knew it was worth it."

"What an ass," our nurse, Heather, muttered.

I could have sworn I heard a giggle come from the other file clerk on staff, Merritt, but when I glanced at the woman sitting at the work station beside me, her head was lowered, her face hidden behind her thick curtain of long, dark hair.

I'd only been here a couple months, but it was just long enough to notice the dynamic between the women was different with Merritt. It wasn't for lack of trying on their part, but Merritt was incredibly quiet and kept to herself. When one of us tried to engage her in conversation, the most we could get out of her were short, whispered answers.

She was nice enough, offering small smiles when we managed to catch her eye, but there was something . . . off. My gut was telling me it wasn't that she was shy; she was trying to hide herself from us, and that left me unsettled.

She looked to be somewhere in her late twenties, and was the only other married woman on staff, so you would have thought this conversation was right up her alley. But she volunteered nothing.

From the corner of my eye, I saw Gretchen and Diana look my way. They were both more than a decade younger than me and in their prime dating years. I didn't have much in common with them, but they were sweet and hilarious, so I didn't mind listening to their stories.

"What do you think, B?" Gretchen asked, pulling my attention away from the computer. "You think she should have put out first?"

I swiveled my chair around to face them. "Absolutely not."

Diana looked at me with curiosity. My friendship with these ladies was mainly surface, so they didn't know much other than that I was married for fifteen years, had three kids, and my husband passed away earlier that year. Because of that, they looked to me like I had all the answers. If only they knew just how unqualified I was to hand out dating advice. "So what should I do?"

I braced one foot on the floor and twisted my chair side to side as I tapped my pen on the desk, thinking her question over. "Personally, I'd hold out for a man who'd want to buy me a lobster dinner simply because he knew I was worth it, not because he expected something in return. And call me old-fashioned, but I believe the first date is too soon to be talking anal. That's more of a fourth or fifth date thing."

Diana and Gretchen burst into laughter just as the mechanical chime above the door went off, filling the lobby with a tinny sound that was a lot less pleasant than an actual bell.

I spun in my chair, the professional smile that had been affixed to my face drooped as I caught sight of the person who'd just come in. Merritt's husband had come into the office once before since I started here. He was the picture of charm and swagger in his expensive suit, his perfectly styled hair, and the gleam of the thick watch on his wrist. He was an attractive man, there was no doubt about it, but something about him didn't sit right with me, despite the attractive toothpaste-commercial-worthy smile. I didn't like him. I'd been around enough to know that the persona he put on was fake, and I had a sinking suspicion that it was masking something dangerous.

He'd gone out of his way to charm the rest of us, even spitting pretty words regarding his wife for his audience, but I didn't miss the way Merritt had curled even deeper in on herself as soon as he walked through the door, or the way her face drained of color. Seeing that had made me watch closer, so I didn't miss the infinitesimal way she flinched when he leaned in to give her a kiss.

He was the same put-together, confident version of himself this time as he moved toward the long counter that separated our section of the office from the rest of the lobby. "Hello, ladies. Hope you're all having a wonderful day." He stopped in front of me since my station was front and center as receptionist, and cast his charismatic smile on each of us. "I just thought I'd surprise my lovely wife with a lunch date."

Diana and Heather cooed over how sweet that was, but while they gave that walking red flag the attention he so clearly craved, I was busy watching Merritt for every little action and reaction. Diana and Heather might have thought it was sweet that a man was swinging by his wife's work to treat her to lunch, but by the way Merritt's complexion turned a ghostly shade of white and her hands fisted so tightly her knuckles bleached, I didn't think she shared in their swooning.

Despite her body's reaction, her lips tilted up into a shy, almost unsure smile as she turned to him. "Thank you, honey. But we're kind of swamped today. I was planning on working through lunch to catch up."

I could have sworn I saw a flash of anger flit across his face before he schooled his features. "Nonsense," he insisted, his charming tone barely masking the command beneath it. "I'm sure your colleagues here would be more than happy to help you out so your husband can spoil you for an hour." His gaze locked with mine, his smile tipping up even higher. "Isn't that right, sweetheart?"

My eyes narrowed and my lips pulled into a tight, flat line. Unlike the other woman around me, I didn't swoon at the bastard. I heard that *sweetheart* for the condescending insult it was meant to be.

I wanted to open my mouth and tell him, "You don't fool me, asshole," but something held me back. I was worried that a man like him wouldn't take kindly to a woman bruising his ego, and I feared what that might mean for Merritt since she was the one who had to go home with him.

Instead of telling him to fuck off like I so desperately wanted to, I gave a single, clipped nod in agreement.

He smiled, but it wasn't a smile of kindness it was one of triumph, like he thought he'd just bested me and gotten his way. It made me like him even less than I already did.

"See?" he chirped happily. "I told you. It's all good."

Merritt's movements were jerky and robotic as she reached for her purse beneath the counter we worked at and stood, heading for the door that led into the waiting area. She smiled up at her husband, but I noticed the way her mouth pulled tight when he reached out and wrapped his fingers around her wrist. Not her hand, her wrist. As though his grip were a shackle, not an affectionate touch. I also didn't miss the way his grip tightened to the point it looked painful. Alarms started going off in my head. I knew this man was dangerous without needing a lick of proof. Unfortunately, without it, there wasn't much I could do to help Merritt.

BETWEEN THE MIND-NUMBING WORK, spending the rest of the day worrying about Merritt, and the fact that I hadn't slept well in months, I was running on fumes by the time I handled school and daycare pickup, and it was barely four in the afternoon.

I would have given anything to take a nice, long soak in a hot tub with a glass of wine then sleep for a full eight hours, but there was still too much to do. I had to make dinner, help Avett and Adeline with their schoolwork, make sure everyone bathed—and by bathed I meant did more than just stand beneath the water for ten minutes before hopping out and declaring they were clean. At 9, 7, and 4, I still had to make sure my kids used soap.

Unfortunately, before I could do any of that, I had to stop at the grocery store. Thanks to all the stress cooking, Tristan's pantry and fridge were running low.

"All right guys, you know the drill," I said as I threw my SUV into park and twisted to look back at my kiddos. "You behave in there and you can each get *one* treat." I held up my index finger for emphasis.

Ainsley did a little happy shuffle. "I wants a princess cupcake!" she declared, and I held back a wince at the thought of the mountain of pink frosting they piled on top of the cupcakes in the bakery section. With that much sugar, I'd be lucky if I got her to sleep before ten.

Adeline's eyes were round with excitement. "Can I have a honeybun?"

I smiled at my oldest daughter. "Sure you can." Then I turned to my boy. "Avett? What are you in the mood for?"

He tapped his chin in contemplation, the picture of seriousness, before stating, "*Technically,* those bags of mini-donuts should count as one since they're all in one bag."

I gave him a look that my mom had given me countless times growing up. My baby boy was sometimes too damn smart for his—and *my*—own good. "Nice try, bud. Push it and I won't let you pick. I'll just get you an oatmeal raisin cookie."

His face screwed up like he'd just sucked on a lemon. "Raisins are gross!"

I arched a brow. "Exactly. So I suggest you play by the rules."

He rolled his eyes, the gesture making him look much older than his nine years. *God, when did my kids start getting so damn big?* "Fine," he let out a beleaguered huff. "I guess I'll get a cake pop."

"Smart man."

I had high hopes that my bribery would make this shopping trip go faster, but I should have known better, because the moment we entered through the retractable glass doors, they started bickering.

"I want to push the cart," Avett proclaimed.

"Nuh-uh! You pushed it last time," Adeline argued. "It's my turn this time."

My son narrowed his eyes at his sister. "No way! You're too little. You can't even see over the handle."

Adeline stomped her foot and clenched her hands into fists. "Can too! Mommy said I had a growth sport and that's why I had to get all new clothes. 'Cause my old ones didn't fit no more."

"It's growth *spurt*," I corrected. "And both of you knock it off. Since you can't play nice, neither of you gets to push the cart." That was followed by a chorus of whiny objections, each of them blaming the other. The twitch in my eyelid sped up.

"Keep arguing and you lose your treats. This is your last warning."

The two of them clamped their mouths shut but continued glaring daggers at each other as I lifted Ainsley and placed her in the seat at the front of the cart and started down the first aisle. We managed to make it down the bread, canned goods, and spices aisles without incident, but my luck ran out two aisles later. I was standing in front of the selection of pastas, trying to decide which would go best with shrimp in a garlic butter sauce when a crash whipped me around.

Avett stood there among what looked like a murder scene, broken glass and marinara sauce splattered everywhere.

He looked up at me with big, remorseful eyes. "Sorry, Momma. I was just tryin' to help and it slipped."

That twitch grew more intense. "That's okay, baby, it was just an accident. But don't move; there's glass everywhere."

Then Rhodes's deep, raspy voice spoke from behind me. "Everything okay?"

How was it that this man always managed to run into me when I was at my worst?

# Chapter Seven

## Blythe

Rhodes strode closer to me and my kids, and with each step he took, I felt my heartrate kick up a little faster. I hadn't really been in the headspace to take him in fully when I ran into him in Lincoln's office, but standing in the middle of the aisle at Fresh Foods, it was impossible to miss how much he'd grown up since I last saw him all those years ago.

I remembered him being so strong when we'd been together. He'd been tall and broad, with arms that made me feel so safe when he held me, but the man standing before me was even bigger. His thighs filled out his dark-washed jeans, and the simple white tee pulled tight across his chest and stretched around his arms, show-casing a walking wall of muscle. There was nothing particularly attractive about jeans and a plain white tee, but somehow, Rhodes made it look almost sinful.

And of course my ex would look gorgeous only the second time I saw him while I was a rumpled, exhausted mess. I was still in my scrubs from work, my hair—which I hadn't even bothered to run a brush through that morning—was thrown up into a sloppy ponytail that was more ratty than artful, and I was pretty sure the mascara I'd swiped on this morning—the only makeup I'd bothered with—was smudged beneath my eyes. Hell, I couldn't even remember if I'd put on deodorant earlier that morning.

I was well and truly a mess while Rhodes looked like the type of man women would walk into traffic for, just to get his attention.

The heavy soles of his motorcycle boots clomped against the floor as he closed the distance between us. "Hey, little man," he started, gracing my son with a straight, white smile. "Had a bit of an accident, huh?" Avett regarded Rhodes curiously but didn't say a word, and I patted myself on the back for having successfully taught my kids not to talk to strangers. "I've been there."

Avett's brown eyes widened. "You have?"

*Looks like I spoke too soon*, I thought to myself.

"Sure. I managed to drop a whole jar of pickles just

last month. Not only did it make a mess, but it stunk too."

Avett let out a little giggle, and the sound froze me to the spot. The sensation that rushed through my chest was somehow pleasant and painful at the same time. That giggle was a good sign. It was a sound I hadn't heard nearly enough over the past several months, so hearing it hurt as much as it healed. It was bittersweet and joyful in one breath.

Ainsley had rebounded well enough after her father's death, but that was to be expected, given her age. But while she was handling it okay, my boy had been struggling.

Avett and Elliott had been so close, and there wasn't a day that passed that he didn't miss his father something fierce. With every loss like the one he'd suffered, a hole formed in his heart that would never fill back up. Some people handled it better than others. Avett was somewhere in the middle. He had his good days and his bad, but I still wished I could take all the bad away for him. I would have gladly added his sadness to everything I was already carrying if it meant I'd have my bright, happy boy back for good.

"I like pickles."

"Me too, buddy. But I like eating 'em. Not smellin' like 'em."

"Yeah," Avett agreed. "They can be kinda stinky."

"Sure can." Rhodes shifted his gaze from my son to me, and being hit with those brown eyes nearly stole the air right out of my lungs. I'd avoided eye contact the whole time I was stuck in that office with him at Alpha Omega, but I hadn't been fast enough this time, and as I stared at my past across the aisle, I felt like I was drowning. The brown was several shades lighter than Avett's and Ainsley's. The flecks of gold and green mixed with the brown made them look almost amber, and I knew from experience that, in the sun, they'd appear to catch fire and take on a shade closer to red clay to match the streaks of auburn in his dark hair. For three years I'd gotten lost in those eyes. For three years I thought those were the only eyes I'd ever love.

I had been wrong.

"You guys need a hand?"

That question snapped me out of my head and back into reality. "We're fine," I insisted. "I just need to find someone who works here—"

I didn't even get the whole sentence out before Rhodes leaned over and scooped Avett up like he weighed next to nothing, plucking out of the center of the spill and depositing him back on the ground at a safe distance.

"Thanks," I said quietly, pushing down the fluttery

feeling in my belly at the sight of Rhodes lifting my son into his arms. I told myself it had nothing to do with him, that I would have had the same reaction to any attractive man hefting my kid about. It wasn't about *Rhodes,* per se. It was simply my body's primal reaction.

Rhodes smiled then, and I took that flutter and began to stomp it to death. "Not a problem at all."

Just then, a woman came scurrying around the end cap and into the aisle. She wore a maroon polo that sported the name of the grocery store on her chest and a pair of khaki pants. "Heard we had a bit of a spill—" Her words died off as I turned to face her fully. Even in a uniform that should have been unflattering, it was impossible not to notice her beauty. She had light brown hair and pale blue eyes, and just enough curves to make me envious. I'd always been bummed I hadn't gotten my mother's ultra-curvy frame, and instead, was willowy. A tense few seconds of silence alerted me to the fact that, while I'd been taking stock of her, her focus had been latched onto the man slowly rising to his full height once again.

"Rhodes," she said in a breath that managed to drip with both pain and longing. "H-hi."

I looked back to Rhodes just in time to catch something that looked a lot like guilt flashing across his features before he blanked it out. "Grace," he greeted with a tilt of his chin and a gentle smile that didn't quite reach his eyes. The tone of his voice wasn't overly friendly, but it wasn't cold either. Just polite enough, like if Goldilocks had to pick a tone that was *just right*. However, I didn't miss the familiarity in his voice that made my stomach feel sour all of a sudden.

"Um . . . how are you? How's Koda?"

"I'm good, thanks. And Koda's Koda. Just living her best life."

Grace's expression changed just then, her features suffusing with a kind of warmth and softness that made me uncomfortable. "That's good. I really miss . . . her." She fumbled over that last word.

Rhodes cleared his throat awkwardly, his gaze ping-ponging between Grace and me so obvious that it drew her attention my way.

She blinked like she hadn't realized I was standing right there the whole time. "Oh, hi!" She replaced her earlier expression with a professional smile.

"Hi. I'm really sorry about the spill."

"Don't sweat it. Happens all the time." She extended her hand for me to shake. "I'm Grace, the manager here."

"I'm Blythe. The mother of these three rug rats."

Her hand spasmed, her fingers squeezing almost to the point of pain as the smile fell right off her face and the color leeched from her cheeks. "Blythe." She said my name like she was familiar with it, but while she seemed to know who I was, I couldn't manage to place her. She looked to be a few years younger, and I scanned my memory bank to see if I could remember her from high school, but there was nothing.

I narrowed my eyes, studying her beautiful face. "Sorry. Do we know each other?"

She blinked then, like she was coming out of some sort of trance, and dropped my hand like my touch scalded her.

"Uh, no." She took a step back, her gaze darting all around. "I'll get someone right over here with a mop to clean this all up.

"Oh. Okay. Well . . . thank you."

She blinked at me for a second before looking back at Rhodes who was standing silent. A flush tinted the tops of his cheeks above the scruff on his face. That longing was even stronger this time before she offered him a quiet goodbye and scurried off without a backward glance. It didn't take a genius to figure out she and Rhodes had history and she very much didn't want it to be in the past, I just didn't know why she looked like she'd seen a ghost when I told her my name.

Adeline's voice broke through the haze of memories I'd almost gotten stuck in. "What's your name?" she asked, looking at Rhodes, as she skipped up beside her big brother.

My middle child had always been the more mindful one. Avett was the brave one, taking his role of big brother extremely seriously. Ainsley was my impulsive one. But Adeline was a planner. She liked to assess every situation before making a decision, and after seeing her brother's acceptance of this man, she'd decided he must have been safe enough. To them, he was. To me, Rhodes Bradbury was anything but safe.

Rhodes crouched, bringing himself to eye-level with my two oldest. The bulky muscle of his thighs tested the strength of the denim they were wrapped in, and I had to silently scold myself to get it together. I had no business noticing his muscles or his smile . . . or his anything. Even if Rhodes and I didn't have a past, it would have been inappropriate. I had more baggage than LAX during the week of Christmas. I needed to focus on getting my shit together and being there for my kids. That should be my *only* focus.

"I'm Rhodes." He held his hand out to Adeline first, then Avett.

"I'm Avett," my son said, puffing his chest out and straightening his shoulders like a little man. "This is my little sister Adeline, and that's Ainsley. And that's my momma." He pointed to the cart I was holding with a death grip, and my youngest—completely oblivious to my turmoil—lifted her hand in a happy wave.

Rhodes's smile grew even bigger as he returned my baby's wave, then his eyes scanned back around, landing on me and pausing briefly before returning to my son. "It's very nice to meet you. And I know your momma." My throat tightened as I tried to brace for what he might say next, but it was no use. He lowered his head just a bit, twisting to look back up at me through an unfairly thick fringe of lashes as he spoke so quietly I nearly missed it. "We used to be friends."

The emotion in those words and in his eyes landed like a gut punch from a heavyweight champion boxer.

Adeline gave a little hop in place. "If you and Mommy are friends, then you should come over for dinner!"

"Honey, that's not—"

Avett chimed in before I could object. "Yeah, you should! Mom's like the best cooker in the whole wide world."

One part of me wanted to squeeze him for the compliment while the other wanted to slap tape over his mouth to get him to be quiet.

"Want to know somethin'?" The two of them nodded with rapt attention. "I used to eat your mom's cookin' all the time." That was another blow. If my ribs kept tightening, I wasn't going to be able to breathe much longer. "And she's the best cook I've ever known. Never met anyone as good as her."

Avett's cheeks grew pink, and his eyes glowed with excitement. "So you'll come, right? I bet she'll make something extra awesome for you."

"Baby, I'm sure he has other things to do."

Rhodes rose to his full height, a good few inches over six feet, and spoke before disappointment could wash over my boy's face. "I'd love to come for dinner." He looked at me, a smile slowly pushing the corners of his mouth upward in a smile.

I narrowed my eyes, trying my hardest to shoot lasers at him as my kids hopped up and down and cheered with excitement that their new buddy could make it to dinner.

And I was stuck, because it was the first time I'd seen the two of them this excited about something in a while, and I didn't have the heart to take it away from them.

Which meant I was stuck having dinner with the first man to ever break my heart.

What fun.

# Chapter Eight

## Rhodes

I knew it was a dick move, jumping at her kids' invitation to dinner when Blythe so clearly didn't want me to go, but I couldn't help myself. When I rounded the corner and saw her standing in the middle of that aisle, it was like every nerve ending in my body sparked to life.

That magnetic pull latched onto me and wouldn't let go. I'd been transfixed. There was nothing particularly sexy about the pale blue scrubs she was wearing, the boxy material hanging loose and hiding her figure, but she was still the most beautiful woman I'd ever laid eyes on. Even with the mascara streaked beneath her eyes.

I'd given myself a moment to soak her in before taking in the chaos swirling around her. Seeing her with her kids felt like taking a baseball bat to the chest. We'd been too young at the time to really understand what it took to be parents, but we'd been so infatuated with each other that we'd talked regularly about starting our life together and what that would look like, and kids had always been a part of the plan. Hell, we'd even gone so far as to pick out names. Seeing the four of them together then was a glaring reminder that she'd managed to do all the things we'd talked about. Only, she'd done them with someone else, because I'd tossed her away.

There was no denying that her kids were cute as hell though. It was obvious the older two took after their father, what with their dark hair and eyes. But there was still some of their mom wrapped up in their features. The youngest, however, was the spitting image of Blythe's mother, Nona, only in toddler form.

I should have minded my own business and walked away right then, left them to their day, but I couldn't. I didn't want to. And I knew that made me an asshole because of everything she was currently dealing with, but I couldn't help myself.

When she'd grudgingly given in to her kids' pleading and invited me to dinner at seven, I'd jumped on the offer, said my goodbyes, and hightailed my ass out of there before she had a chance to change her mind or I had another run-in with Grace.

I'd never meant to hurt Grace. She was a good

woman. I just didn't feel the same way about her that she'd felt for me. I tried, really, but in the end, I called it off because I knew she deserved better. I never lied to her when we were together. Like the few other women I had attempted to get serious with, Grace knew about my past. And she knew about Blythe. We'd had more than one fight about her during the few months we dated. Grace accused me of keeping myself closed off and loved to throw out that I couldn't give her more because I was still hung up on the past. I never once bothered denying it, because she'd been right. My heart had never stopped belonging to Blythe.

I could practically see the knife sinking into her chest earlier when Blythe introduced herself, and I hated that it caused her pain, but there wasn't any way for me to take it away from her.

The problem with living and dating in a small town was there was really no escaping your ex, unless one of you picked up and moved away. Grace hadn't hidden the fact that she'd taken the breakup hard, and I knew from the random texts I still received months after we ended that she was trying to keep herself in my mind, hoping I would eventually realize what I let go. Unfortunately, that was never going to happen, even before Blythe's return.

I shook off thoughts of my ex as I pressed on the

brake pedal, slowing my truck to a stop in front of Tristan Fanning's house. Blythe had scrawled her brother's address on the back of a receipt she dug out of her purse back at Fresh Foods, but I already knew exactly where he lived. I knew where all of Blythe's family was. I knew it made me seem creepy as hell, but I'd even kept track of everyone important to her. I knew her parents' address by heart. I knew her half-brother, Liam, had gone to college in Edinburgh and loved it so much he decided to make that his home base. I knew that her step-brother, Shawn, was living in Arizona with his family, and that Hannah, her step-sister was over in Kentucky.

I'd been torturing myself for two fucking decades, asking Sunny questions I knew the answers to would kill me, but at this point, it was a compulsion. An addiction that had long since burrowed beneath my skin.

I'd taken the time to change before heading over, dressing in a pair of jeans that weren't thread-bare and faded, and I'd traded my T-shirt in for a plaid button-down that I kept untucked and cuffed the sleeves up my forearms. The only thing that stayed were my motor-cycle boots. Aside from my running shoes, they were the only other pair of shoes I owned. But as I glanced down at them I wished I would have at least taken the time to shine them up a bit.

"Oh, well," I huffed out on a quiet breath. "Too late now."

Grabbing the bottle of wine I'd picked up on my way here, I climbed out of my truck and beeped the locks before heading up the walkway.

As soon as I pressed the doorbell, I heard a burst of commotion from inside. A dog started barking like crazy, the sound growing closer before it ended with a heavy *thud* that rattled the door.

I heard a little boy voice call out, "I got it!" right before I heard the scrape of the deadbolt and the door was thrown open.

Blythe was clearly mid-lecture as her son opened the door for me, and I caught, "—told you over and over, you can't open the door." She jerked to a stop as she stepped into the living room, the dishtowel she'd been drying her hands with frozen in her grip as soon as she caught sight of me standing in the open doorway. "Uh, hi."

"You came!" Avett exclaimed, oblivious to the chewing out he'd been getting from his mom only seconds earlier.

I grinned down at him. "Of course I came. Not gonna turn down an invitation from a guy as cool as you."

His chest puffed out visibly, his shoulders pushing back as his cheeks bloomed red with pride. He shot me a snaggle-toothed grin that reminded me so much of my nephew Cooper's, only he was missing more teeth and from different places.

"Ave, buddy. Why don't you move out of the doorway and let Rhodes come in, huh? Unless you want him to eat dinner on the front stoop."

"Oh, yeah." He stepped back and to the side to make room for me. I reached down to ruffle his hair as I stepped inside. "Thanks, big man."

The dog, probably suffering from head trauma, started sniffing at my shoes and jeans, most likely smelling my dog, Koda, on me.

I bent down to give it a pat, taking it in. "Jesus," I grunted. It didn't look like any dog I'd ever seen before. "What is that thing?"

"That's Doc," Avett stated. "He's Uncle Tris's dog. Mom says he's a little sissy bi—"

"Avett!" Blythe snapped before he could finish, her face red with embarrassment.

The kid looked back at his mom, a sheepish smile on his face. "Sorry, Momma." Then he turned back to me with a serious expression. "But he kinda is. If he doesn't eat at the same time every day, he rolls over on his back and howls like he's dyin', and when Uncle Tris tried to clip his claws, he passed out."

I glanced in Blythe's direction. "Didn't realize dogs could pass out."

She draped the dish towel over her shoulder and crossed her arms over her chest. "Neither did I. Until I met that stumpy little diva."

Just then the tiny redhead came flying down the stairs at a speed that nearly gave me a heart attack. I took an instinctive step forward just as she jumped from the second to last step, worried about another head injury in this house. Fortunately, she landed safely on her tiny, bare feet.

She skidded to a stop in front of me and lifted her short arms over her head to show me the large, rainbow-colored stuffed animal in her hands. "I'm Ainsley, and this is my unicorn, Jerry," she announced, pronouncing her THs as Ds and her Rs like Ws.

My brows went up at the same time my smile widened. "Jerry, huh? Is that a common name for a unicorn?"

She lifted her shoulders in a shrug and looked at me like that was the stupidest question she'd ever heard. "I dunno. He's the only one I know."

Christ, she was adorable. "Well, Jerry's a very hand-some unicorn."

That seemed to make her happy, and she grinned so big her chubby cheeks nearly squished her eyes closed, then she was skipping off as quickly as she appeared, dragging Jerry along behind her.

I twisted my head to look at Blythe and raised my eyebrows. "*Jerry?*"

She shrugged, the mannerism the exact same as what her daughter had just done. "That one's been headstrong since she came out of the womb. She gets something in her mind, she won't be swayed. She heard the name Jerry somewhere, liked it, and that was that." She came closer and lifted her hand, placing it on the top of her son's head. "Why don't you take Doc out to the backyard and let him run around a bit? Keep an eye out, make sure he didn't give himself a concussion bashing into that door."

"Yes, ma'am," he said before letting out a whistle and patting his thigh to get the stocky dog to chase after him.

"I brought this," I said, lifting the bottle of wine I was still clutching as a wave of nerves crashed into me. It wasn't lost on me that this was the closest Blythe and I had been in twenty years, and you would have thought by the way my stomach was twisting and my skin was tingling, like it was suddenly too tight for my skeleton, that I was a clueless virgin alone with a girl for the very first time.

"I, um, hope it's okay. I wasn't sure if you preferred red or white."

"Yes," she answered, snatching the bottle from me like a kid going after the last piece of cake. My mouth fell open on a rusty laugh. I hadn't forgotten her dry sense of humor, but it was different, hearing it again for the first time in so long. "Come on in. I'll open this up, and maybe I can be talked into sharing."

I let loose another chuckle. "Sounds like you need that more than I do."

She cast a glance at me over her shoulder, those turquoise eyes flashing. "It's a day ending in Y, so, yeah, I need it." She meant it to come off as a joke, but my chest still clenched as I remembered that she was doing this all alone and why, due to everything she'd lost recently. I didn't know how the hell she was still standing, let along functioning. Then again, Blythe had always been so damn strong.

I closed the door and trailed after her, my gaze moving down and taking her in. She'd changed out of her scrubs into a pair of cropped jeans and a T-shirt that sported the name of the university she attended on the front in faded burgundy letters. Her denims looked at least a size too big for her, but I could still make out the roundness of her heart-shaped ass as I followed behind her like an eager puppy. I noticed her feet were bare and her toes were painted a vibrant, tropical pink. Her hair was down now, but untamed, the strands somewhere between wavy and curly, and all wild.

She was dressed for comfort, for a night at home with her family. Nothing about her screamed that she'd put much effort into her appearance because it wasn't necessary. She was effortlessly beautiful, even with the faint smudges beneath her eyes that I could tell she tried to hide with a bit of makeup.

The house smelled like heaven. The scent of garlic and herbs permeated the air, creating an aroma that made my stomach growl, reminding me I hadn't eaten anything since the protein shake and banana I had for breakfast.

Blythe had always been a master in the kitchen—her cooking rivaling even Detty's—and I couldn't believe I was finally getting the chance to taste it again.

# Chapter Nine

## Blythe

I lifted my wineglass to my lips for a sip, only to discover it was already empty. If I didn't slow down, I was going to get drunk, and I needed to keep my wits about me, at least as long as Rhodes was in my house—or, rather, my brother's house.

Dinner had consisted of chicken enchiladas—one of the meals that had been taking up space in Tristan's freezer—homemade Spanish rice, and charro beans. My kids managed to make a dent in the meal, and with Rhodes here, there wasn't a leftover in sight, so maybe my brother would finally quit bitching about my stress cooking and his lack of freezer space.

Sitting at the kitchen table with him and my kids was . . . surreal. There was no other word to describe it. I'd been convinced I would never see this man again, and now we'd managed to share a meal. I couldn't say the evening had been comfortable, but it hadn't been the worst.

The conversation between the two of us might have been stilted, but between my three kids, they managed to keep things from getting too awkward. It was clear that Ainsley liked Rhodes, but then, my baby girl liked everyone. It was Avett and Adeline I was most surprised by—Addy, especially. Avett was a friendly kid, but he was usually so into his own thing that it took a lot for someone to catch his interest the way Rhodes had.

While Adeline was quieter about it, as was her way, I could see her curiosity in Rhodes had been piqued, and she'd spent dinner asking questions, trying to get to know him.

More than once I wished that Tristan didn't have to work late, knowing his presence would act as the barrier I needed between Rhodes and me, because, like my kids, I was way too curious about the man sitting across from me. And if history had taught me anything, having those feelings would lead nowhere good.

I had no business wanting to know more, wanting to dig deeper and see what the past two decades had been like for Rhodes. That interest should have been severed when he told me we didn't have a future before walking away from me for good. But I wanted to know what his life was like now. I wanted to know about his time in the Army, and how long he'd been out. I wanted to know if working for Lincoln was everything he used to think it would be. I knew that being a part of the Alpha Omega team had always been a dream of his, then, as he got older, a goal he was determined to work toward. Despite how badly he'd hurt me, and how much I wanted not to care, I was still happy to see he'd made that particular dream come true.

I'd made a conscious effort for years not to ask my best friend, Sunny, about her oldest brother. I'd made her promise never to bring his name up. At first it was out of spite, then necessity. After enough time had passed, I convinced myself I didn't care. I had a life of my own, a good one, and there was no room for Rhodes Bradbury.

If only I'd been able to get the damn man out of my head. Unfortunately, no matter how hard I tried, thoughts of him managed to creep up when I least expected it. It wasn't that I didn't love Elliott. I really did, I just couldn't stop my brain from making comparisons every now and then.

Guilt ate away at me whenever that happened. I felt like the worst wife in the entire world, simply because of thoughts I had no control over. Who knew my husband never suffered from the same crisis of conscience.

"So, you were like, a real-life soldier?"

Avett's question pulled me out of the past, and I set my empty wineglass on the table, pushing it back so I wouldn't be tempted to pour a third glass, and leaned forward in my seat to better hear Rhodes's answer.

"Yeah, little man. I was a real-life soldier."

His eyes went bigger. "What was it like?"

Adeline chimed in then. "Did you ever have to deal with bad guys?"

That caught Ainsley's attention. "Was it scary?"

Rhodes chuckled like he was taking their questions in stride, but I didn't miss the way the skin around his eyes tightened with discomfort.

"It was scary at times, yeah. And unfortunately, I did have to deal with some bad guys. But I signed up for that because I wanted to help keep people safe. It was important to me, and that's exactly what I did."

Something told me there was a lot more he wasn't saying, but it wasn't my place to push, not anymore. No matter how badly I might have wanted to know.

"Cool," Avett said on a breath. "I wanna be a soldier when I'm grown up."

The tines of my fork scraped loudly across my plate at that declaration, every muscle in my body growing tight as fear knitted around my lungs and squeezed. The past six months had been bad enough. I didn't need my kids trying to force me into cardiac arrest.

"Why don't we talk about what you're going to be when you grow up in another decade," I suggested. "By then maybe you'll see the value of being an accountant. Or a dentist." I never heard of a dentist dying on the job.

His face scrunched up, the holes from his missing teeth reminding me he was still my little boy—at least for a little while longer. "No way! Dentists are the *worst*. And I don't wanna have to smell people's stinky breath every day."

He had me there. Looked like I was going to have to push the accountant gig hard when he got older.

"I'm gonna train tigers when I grow up!" Ainsley proclaimed loudly.

I dropped my fork onto my plate. "Okay. How about you guys clear the table before you give your mom a heart attack? Dishes in the sink, then you can have thirty minutes of screen time before showers."

They grumbled as they cleared the table, but they still did it, so I considered that a win.

As soon as the dishes had been dumped in the sink, the three of them took off to different parts of the house. I didn't realize my mistake until Rhodes came into the kitchen behind me, carrying his own plate and wine glass as I turned on the water.

"There anything I can help with?" he asked, his presence shrinking the space around us. That had always been the case when we were younger. There was just something about him that filled all the tiny spaces in every room he entered. His presence was unavoidable and intoxicating. He'd been formidable when we were kids, and that had only grown stronger since. I didn't think I could handle being alone with him for any amount of time.

"Oh, no. That's not necessary." I cast a small smile over my shoulder, hoping it didn't look as fake as it felt. "I'm sure you've got better things to do—"

I knew he wasn't going to make this easy on me when he pushed his sleeves up, revealing even more of those thickly carved forearms. "Not at all. Besides, you cooked, it's not fair for you to have to handle cleanup too."

Something painful stabbed into the center of my chest. A familiar burn formed behind my eyes as I lowered my head and stared down into the sink. With Elliott's betrayal having come to light, it was easy to lose sight of all that I had truly lost, but it was times like this that I was reminded, when the good of the past slammed into me like a freight train.

Elliott had always insisted on cleaning up after dinner. I cooked, he cleaned, that was how it had always worked. Until it didn't. Until I lost *my* partner, the person who had always been there to help me carry the burden so I didn't have to do it alone.

"Hey." Rhodes' gentle voice yanked me out of my memories. He laid a hand on my arm, wrapping his fingers around my bicep tenderly to turn me toward him. "What just happened? Did I say something wrong?"

I sniffled, wiping my nose with the back of my hand as I shook my head. I caught the briefest glimpse of concern in his amber eyes, and it only made the tightness in my chest that much worse.

"No, it's nothing. Really. I'm fine. It's just . . ."

His finger came beneath my chin, lifting my gaze to his. It was something he'd done when we were together, whenever he wanted my attention on him, and the movement was so familiar it was painful.

"It's just what? Blythe, talk to me. You can tell me anything."

I pushed down the ache his sweetness caused. I couldn't focus on that or I'd lose the already-fragile hold I had on everything, sending me spiraling. I couldn't afford to spiral, not when I was all my kids had left.

"Ever since I found those pictures . . ." I had to stop to swallow down the sickly taste of bile that slithered up my throat at the thought of those *fucking* pictures. "Since then, I've been so angry I've forgotten to be sad."

I shook my head and let out a sigh. "Then something will happen and I'll remember that before I was mad, I was heartbroken."

The look in his eyes was bad enough, but when he breathed out, "Angel," it nearly killed me.

I took a step back, breaking contact. "Don't," I said in a ragged whisper.

*Angel* was what he'd given to me when we were together, when we were so in love we were all the other could see. *Angel* was special. It meant something. And he'd taken it away. He couldn't just use it again whenever he felt like it.

"Don't do that. Don't call me that. Just . . . don't. Please."

He dropped his arm, his hands clenching into white-knuckled fists at his sides. When he spoke, his tone was like gravel. "I'm sorry."

I nodded, not trusting my voice not to betray every little thing I was feeling. We worked in silence for a while, side by side. I rinsed the dishes and passed them to him to be loaded into the dishwasher. The tension in the air was so thick it could have been cut with the knife Rhodes just loaded.

It took a while, but I finally managed to muster up the courage to ask the question that had been weighing on my mind all evening. Hell, if I was being honest, it was the question I'd had on my mind for days.

"Have you, um, have you found . . . anything?"

Rhodes let out a breath that had me turning my head in his direction. It appeared it was his turn to avoid eye contact. "I thought it would be better if Linc took lead on that. I didn't . . ." Those amber eyes of his landed back on me. "I thought you might prefer if it was him."

I didn't have the first clue how to feel about that. There was relief, then there was disappointment that I couldn't even begin to understand. Instead of saying anything, I nodded, and we went back to silence.

It was the easiest way with us.

# Chapter Ten

## Blythe

The morning at the clinic had been packed with back to back clients, and things had been moving at such a fast pace there hadn't been a chance for me to speak with Merritt. I'd been trying to talk to her more to see if I could get her to come out of her shell. Truth was, I was worried about her. I could have sworn I saw a bruise on her hip the other day. She'd been reaching up to slide a file back into place on one of the higher shelves, causing her scrubs top to ride up a bit, but before I could be certain it was a bruise and not just a shadow, she jerked it back in place.

The mechanical chime of the door sounded, and I looked up as Ivy Young came through, followed closely by her boyfriend, Connor. The two of them were much more touchy-feely now than they had been when she first started coming to see Dr. Shaundry. I hadn't asked, not wanting to dig into business that wasn't mine, but it was clear that the pregnancy had been an accident. As the big man placed his hand on the small of Ivy's back and guided her to the reception desk, all while looking down at her like she was the very thing that hung the moon in the sky each night, I was glad to see they'd made it through the rough patches and appeared to be going strong.

Ivy smiled brightly as she stopped across the counter from me, placing a palm on the swell of her belly. She hadn't been showing the last time she came in, but now it was obvious that her rounded belly was more than just an extra-large burrito for lunch.

"Hi," she greeted me, looking happy and healthy and so much brighter than the last time I'd seen her.

I returned her smile with one of my own. "Wow, look at you."

"I know." Her hand caressed her stomach affectionately. "It was the weirdest thing. I just kind of popped overnight."

"Yeah, it'll happen like that. But it looks good on you."

Connor drew closer to her like he couldn't stand even the smallest distance between them. Looping his arm over her shoulder, he pulled her into his side to press a kiss to her temple. "Didn't think it was possible for her to get more beautiful than she already was, but then she went and proved me wrong."

The genuine adoration in his eyes as he gazed at her was beautiful and painful to witness at the same time. I was so incredibly happy for Ivy that she was happy. She was a good person. She'd reached out more than once not long after I returned to Hope Valley, but I hadn't been in a very good place then. She deserved her happily ever after, and I did everything in my power to stomp down the pang of envy trying to spring to life at the realization that, not only had I lost my happily ever after, but it had all been a lie in the first place.

"Have a seat and I'll let them know you're here. Heather will be out to take you back in just a minute."

"Thanks, Blythe."

Ivy took the hand Connor extended and let him lead her to one of the cushy chairs lining the walls. As I swiveled my chair around to face my computer, I caught Merritt looking out into the waiting room, sadness chiseled into the plains of her face and glistening from her eyes.

My ribs squeezed tight in my chest as I watched her watching Ivy and Connor. If I hadn't already suspected something was very wrong in her marriage, the way she looked just then would have been all the confirmation I needed.

She blinked, her eyes clearing and the mask falling back into place. A small, shaky grin pulled at her mouth when she caught me staring. "They're a cute couple," she said with a sniffle before whipping back around to face her computer screen.

I reached over, placing a hand on her arm. "Honey, are you okay?"

She nodded a bit frantically. "Yeah. Sure. I'm all good."

There wasn't an ounce of truth to those words. "Okay, but you know, if you ever need to talk, I'm here." It was a pitiful offer, one so much smaller than what I really wanted to give her, but if I pushed too fast, I knew she'd lock down, then there'd be no chance of helping her.

The rest of the day was uneventful and a bit dull, only livening up once I picked up my kids from school and daycare. Listening to them chatter on about their day was always a highlight of mine. Hearing them talk about their friends gave me a small glimmer of hope that I hadn't screwed everything up by uprooting their lives and moving them out here so soon after losing their father.

"Look!" Adeline's arm shot between the front seats

as I turned my SUV into the driveway. "Uncle Tris is home!"

Sure enough, his truck was parked in the driveway, marking the first time in weeks he'd been home before the sun went down. We'd been living with my little brother for months, but with his work schedule and the havoc in my life, I felt like I hardly saw him. We'd been separated by states for years, but recently I'd missed him more than I had in all that time.

The front door opened as I hefted Ainsley out of her booster and placed her on the ground. All three of my kids bolted toward their uncle. "Hey, guys," he chuckled as a tiny tornado of kids descended upon him. All three of them were talking over each other, vying for his attention, to the point of yelling.

"Good lord, guys. Let your uncle breathe for a second, why don't you?"

He placed his hands on top of Adeline's and Avett's heads and smiled down at them. "Doc's out back runnin' through the sprinkler I set up. Why don't you guys go join him? I'll be right out. I need to talk to your momma first."

The kids took off like a bullet, eager to play in the water with Tristan's dog. Meanwhile, my stomach sank at the emotion skating over my brother's face as he looked back up at me.

"What's up?" I managed to ask, though everything inside me was screaming that I didn't want to know. "You got really serious all of a sudden."

He braced his hands on his hips and lowered his head as he let out a gust of breath. "I tried callin'. Wanted to give you a heads-up."

"You're freaking me out, little bro. Just tell me, already."

I knew what was coming as soon as I saw the sympathy in his eyes, but I found myself holding my breath anyway. "Lincoln's here to see you, B."

And there it was.

It was funny how I'd been preparing myself for this very thing, yet I still wasn't prepared.

I COULDN'T BREATHE. As I stumbled out of the house and onto the front stoop, I struggled to fill my lungs with air. It felt like someone had punched me right in the stomach, knocking the wind out of me. I guess, given the news I just received, that was about right.

Footsteps sounded behind me, just as Tristan's voice called out. "B? You okay?"

I wasn't. God, I was the furthest thing from okay. "I

can't—" My voice cracked, and it took everything in me not to burst into tears. I didn't want my kids to see me break down. They needed their mother to be strong. I couldn't crumble. Not again. Elliott had caused that too many times already.

"I can't be here," I finally managed to get out. "Can you—?"

"Of course. I've got the kids, B. You do what you need to do. I'm here. I'm always here."

I nodded, blinking back the burn in my eyes as I raised up on my toes and pressed a kiss to his cheek. "Thanks," I croaked, that single word scraping along my throat like sandpaper. I rushed to my car and threw it into gear. I wanted to slam on the gas pedal and take off, but that would have been reckless, and reckless wasn't something my family could afford.

I didn't know where the hell I was going, but I couldn't stay in that house, not with the walls closing in on me after the bomb Lincoln dropped.

It hadn't been an affair. It was so much worse.

It hurt bad enough to know my husband had been sleeping with someone else, but he'd built a whole life I didn't know about. Knowing he had a whole other *family* . . . well, that killed. He had two kids with her, for Christ's sake. *Kids*! All those business trips, all those lectures and conferences I thought he was going to, those had all been a cover for him to go spend time with them. His second family.

The pain in my chest wouldn't let up. It was so bad that, if I hadn't known better, I would have thought I was having a heart attack. What I was dealing with might not have been life threatening, but my heart was irreparably damaged nonetheless.

I ended up somewhere I hadn't been in years, somewhere I never expected to be again. I'd driven on autopilot to a place that used to be second nature to me. Still dressed in my scrubs and hospital approved shoes from work, this definitely was not the proper footwear to be wearing on a hike, but my body moved of its own accord, without any input from my brain. Before I knew what was happening, I was out of my SUV and starting up a trail I used to know like the back of my hand.

My feet slipped on the bed of fallen leaves on the soft ground. I wound through the trees, somehow managing to keep from falling as I moved up, up, up. The tightness in my chest refused to loosen its vise grip. I was dangerously close to hyperventilating as I burst through the trees into the clearing beyond.

This place had meant something back then. It was special. It was a place Rhodes and I had kept to ourselves. It was where we'd first kissed, where I'd given him my virginity, where he'd said he loved me for the first time, and where he'd told me he planned on joining the Army as soon as he graduated, but I wasn't focused on any of that then.

The cliff overlooked the beauty of this valley. It was a view that never failed to take my breath away with its stunning vista, but now I wasn't seeing any of it. I couldn't hear the trickle of the river below over the rush of blood in my ears. I couldn't appreciate the peaks and valleys of the mountains stretched out before me. All I could think about was the pressure building inside of me. I felt like my insides were made of that shit kids put in their science fair volcanos, just waiting to explode. I was a human pressure cooker, and if I didn't find some way to release it, I was going to lose my mind.

So I did the only thing I could think to do. It was the very thing Tristan had suggested days ago. I leaned back, opened my mouth, and screamed as loud and long as I possibly could. I felt better afterward, so I did it again. And again. Until my throat felt like it was on fire and tears were streaming down my face. Once I couldn't scream any longer, I started letting out a stream of curses in between broken sobs as I poured out all the pain eating me up inside.

I sucked in a gasp and whipped around at the snap of a twig, right to where Rhodes was standing between two wide oak trees.

"Of course!" I shouted up at the sky, throwing my arms out wide. "Of *course* you're here right now. How is it you always pop up when I'm at my very worst, huh? Did I do something evil in a past life? Was I an auditor for the IRS or something?"

Before he could formulate an answer, a fresh wave of rage and sorrow crashed into me, taking me down to my knees as my tears fell and leached into the dirt beneath me.

# Chapter Eleven

## Rhodes

She was the last person I expected to see when I came up to the lookout.

*Our* lookout.

It had been our place when we were together, and since getting out of the Army and coming back home, it had become my sanctuary. It was where I went when I needed to think, when I needed a break from the real world. I came here today because I knew Lincoln was going to tell Blythe about what he found, and it was the only place I could think to come to ease the ache in my chest at the thought of how that news was going to destroy her.

Knowing what was about to happen, and that there was nothing I could do to make it any better for her, left me feeling helpless, an emotion I didn't handle well. I'd been helpless when it came to stopping my parents from bailing on us. Helpless whenever anything in that piece-of-shit trailer we'd grown up in broke down on us. Helpless to stop my own sister from having to take her clothes off and dance for money to make sure she kept a roof over our heads.

I'd felt helpless in school when the kids would make fun of us for being poor trailer trash, and that helplessness had led to destruction. Once I was big enough to hold my own, I'd gotten into my fair share of fights with the assholes who insulted any member of my family or made disgusting comments about Gypsy being a stripper. I'd gotten really good at fighting back then, and even better at not getting caught. It helped that the jackasses I beat the shit out of didn't want to admit they'd gotten their asses handed to them by the poor kid from the wrong side of the tracks.

I didn't want my big sister to know I'd been fighting. That would have only added more stress on top of everything else she had to carry. The only person who knew was Blythe, and she never said a word. She'd just silently take care of me, disinfecting the cuts or scrapes I received or bandaging my knuckles, all without an ounce of judgement.

That was why I'd fallen in love with her. She had been the only safe place I had to fall back on, and the fact that I couldn't be there to offer the same thing when she found out the truth tore me up inside.

That was why I'd come to the lookout. I came out here so much that this place was almost as familiar to me as my own home. I spent more nights than I could count up here, falling asleep with my back propped against the very tree I used to rest against while I held Blythe between my legs, the two of us content to stare in silence as the sun dipped behind the jagged peaks of the mountain tops. Being here let me feel like I was still close to her. The memories we'd shared here had seeped into the dirt and rock and taken root, breathing life into the trees and leaves and grass.

She was the very last person I expected to see when I breached the treeline to the clearing fifty yards from the edge of the cliff, but there was a part of me that wasn't surprised she managed to find her way back here. That same part sparked with hope that the lookout still meant something to her as well. However, that hope shriveled and died with her first agonized scream.

With every sob, every scream, every tear that fell, she cut away a piece of my heart I knew I would never get back. Her pain became my own, the pressure in my chest so heavy it was nearly unbearable. I stood there until I couldn't take it for another second.

I probably should have left her alone, turned around and left the way I came, but I couldn't do it. I couldn't stand by and watch her suffer alone like that.

The twig snapping beneath my boot might as well have been a shotgun blast.

She spun around, her turquoise eyes red and shimmering with unshed tears. "Of course!" she shouted in frustration, tipping her head back to the sky. "Of *course* you're here right now. How is it you always pop up when I'm at my very worst, huh? Did I do something evil in a past life? Was I an auditor for the IRS or something?"

I opened my mouth to respond, but before I could get a word out, her face pinched up all over again and she went down to her knees on the unforgiving ground as sobs wracked her body. I couldn't stand there and watch any longer. Seeing her like that fucking killed me.

I moved before my brain could fully register what was happening. One second I was watching from a distance and the next I was dropping down beside her, wrapping her in my arms, and pulling her into my lap in a desperate attempt to absorb some of the torment she was feeling. I would have given anything to take it all away, to carry that burden on my own so she didn't have to. I'd hated Elliott from the moment Sunny told me Blythe met someone in college she'd gotten serious about. I never met the man, but I hated him for the simple fact that he had the woman I wanted with every fiber of my being.

It wasn't his fault. I'd been the one to throw everything we were away. But I still hated him for being the one to put her pieces back together. I'd been in the middle of the desert a world away when I found out he'd proposed and she'd said yes, and when the day of their wedding rolled around, a few buddies from my unit took me out to get wasted. Those had been the worst days of my life, and on top of blaming myself for losing her, I also blamed the man who now had her.

However, as Blythe's tears soaked through my shirt and her back heaved beneath my hands, I couldn't help but wish I could bring that piece of shit back to life so I could kill him all over again.

All these years, I'd managed to take the smallest amount of comfort in the fact that at least Blythe had someone who loved her and took care of her. Someone to give her all the things I never felt I was good enough to give her myself. To find out that had all been a lie was a serious blow, so I couldn't imagine how it felt for her.

I lost track of how long we sat there, me offering silent comfort and her taking it, but by the time her sobs had tapered off into sniffles, the sun was lower in the sky, the very bottom of it kissing the tops of the mountains as it began its descent.

"You knew." Her voice was ragged and throaty, like she'd been gargling gravel.

It wasn't a question, so I didn't bother lying. "I did."

She pulled back, wiping at her swollen eyes, and as hard as it was, I forced myself to let her go. The sense of loss as she slid off my lap was so profound it stole the breath from my lungs. I wanted to reach out and pull her back, but I didn't have the right to. Instead, I rose to my feet at the same time she did and shoved my hands in the pockets of my jeans as she moved closer to the cliff's edge and stared at the gorgeous view.

"But you sent Linc to tell me anyway."

"I didn't think you would want to hear it from me."

Her back expanded on a deep inhale. "You were right." The words were barely more than a whisper caught on the breeze and carried to me. "This is bad enough. The humiliation . . ." She dropped her head, giving it a shake.

"Hey, stop that," I clipped, unable to maintain the distance between us. Moving beside her, I tucked my finger beneath her chin and lifted her face to mine. The way her eyes glistened and her chin trembled hurt worse than any hit I'd ever taken. And I had taken some serious fucking hits in my life. "You have nothing to be humiliated about, you hear me? *Nothing*."

A tiny whimper crept past her lips as a single tear welled and slipped down her cheek. "I don't understand," she said quietly, sadness winding and knotting around her words. "Why has every man I've ever loved hurt me? What is so wrong with me that I can't just be loved back?" She blinked and dealt the death blow with one last question. "Why am I not good enough?"

I'd done some shitty things in my life. Things I wasn't proud of, things that left me disappointed and mad at myself. But for the first time in my life, I well and truly hated myself. Because I had a hand in making her feel that way.

Unworthy of being loved.

Undeserving.

I'd felt that way more times than I could count. It was easy to believe when your own parents didn't love you enough to stick around. But making Blythe feel that? I would never forgive myself.

She was the one person on this planet I knew deserved nothing but good days and happiness.

"Angel, you're breaking my fuckin' heart." My throat tightened as I stretched my fingers out and pressed my palm to the side of her neck, caressing her silky skin gently. "There isn't a single thing wrong with you. You are perfect." I stepped closer, bringing my other hand up to brush her wild hair back from her eyes and cup her cheek.

"Then why?" she rasped as a wave of silent tears started to fall.

I knew what she was asking. She wasn't asking me why her father had chosen drugs and crime over her. She wasn't asking why her husband had betrayed the vows he'd taken. She didn't want me to tell her why those men hurt her. She was asking why *I* had.

"Because I was the one who was broken, Angel. It was me who didn't deserve you. I knew from the moment you gave me your heart I wasn't good enough." I squeezed my eyes closed and lowered my head, resting my forehead against hers. Her small hands came up and pressed against my chest, burning my skin like a brand. It was a searing pain that somehow felt overwhelming and incredible at the same time, and I would have gladly felt that way every single day of my life if it meant staying connected with her. "You were all that was good in the world. You were light and beauty and happiness."

Her fingers curled, her nails scraping across my pecs as she fisted the fabric of my shirt.

"You are more than good enough. You're more than deserving of love, and I know that because I've never stopped. Even after I broke us, I never stopped loving you. Not for a single second of a single minute in a single day."

She pulled in a gasping breath, her head tilting back so her eyes could meet mine. Those Caribbean blue depths were full of shock and confusion. It probably wasn't the right time to tell her that after everything she'd already been through today—or hell, the past several months—but I couldn't go another second with her thinking she wasn't worthy of love. She had to know she was special. She was worth waiting an eternity for.

"Rhodes," she whispered. My name on those lips was a blessing and a curse all at once. The way she was looking up at me made me feel like the most important person in the world. I felt that undeniable tug grow stronger, giving me no choice but to get closer to her. It wasn't a want, it was a need—like oxygen or water. Blythe was essential to living. That was why I'd only led half an existence since letting her go.

More and more of the distance between us disappeared as my eyes dropped to her lips. That plump bottom lip called to me, begging to be nipped and licked. "Angel."

She blinked, and I saw the instant the bubble around us burst right before she took a step back from me. For the shortest moment, her guard had fallen, but as I watched, she re-erected those protective walls of hers and coated them in the same shit Captain America's shield was made of.

"I—I have to go."

I stood rooted to the ground as I watched her disappear into the trees, and I knew beyond a shadow of a doubt that watching her walk away from me was something I would never get used to.

# Chapter Twelve

### Blythe

I couldn't remember the last time I felt this exhausted. I was wrung out, emotionally and physically. Everything hurt.

I'd texted Tristan to make sure it was okay to leave the kids with him for the night as soon as I got back to my car, and after he replied that he had everything covered, I drove to the opposite side of town.

My brother must have called in advance and told her everything, because my mother was already sitting out on her front porch by the time I turned my SUV into her driveway. I thought I was all cried out, but the second I saw her the tears started all over again. Mom stood from the top step as I climbed out of the car and rounded the hood.

"Mommy—"

My voice broke on that one word, my face crumpling into a sob.

Tears filled her eyes as she opened her arms. "Oh, my honey pie. Come here."

I threw myself into her arms and let her hold me as I let it all out for the second time in just a matter of hours. But at least in her arms, I knew I was safe. As she held me, a sense of comfort washed over me that this was exactly where I needed to be to start healing.

Stepping into the break room, I headed straight for the fancy coffee maker Dr. Shaundry had purchased for us and set about making my second cup of the morning. I was going to need it. After the emotional upheaval of the day before, I was running on fumes. I'd cried on my mother's shoulder until I finally passed out, spending the night on her oversized sectional couch, but even eight uninterrupted hours hadn't been enough to shake off the exhaustion. It was going to be a three-cup day, at least, if I didn't want to fall asleep at my desk.

I was watching the stream of the dark liquid drip into my mug when I caught movement from the corner of my eye.

"Good morning," Merritt offered as she moved to the fridge to stow away her lunch.

"Morning," I returned, my smile feeling tight, given that most of my face was still a bit swollen from my crying jag. I knew the half-hearted job with concealer I'd attempted this morning had been a waste when I saw her eyes widen as she took me in.

"Are—" She swallowed, and I could see the uncertainty in her pretty face before she pushed past it to ask, "Are you all right?"

I could have lied and given some boilerplate response. Something along the lines of "Oh, yeah. I'm fine," or, "I just didn't sleep well last night," but as I took her in, it hit me that the truth might be a way in.

"At the moment, no. I'm feeling especially shitty right now, but I'm hopeful I'll be okay eventually."

She rocked back on her heel, my answer clearly not what she'd been expecting to hear.

The coffee machine sputtered before beeping, letting me know my coffee was finished, and I didn't hesitate to pick it up and take a sip.

"I—um . . . I'm sorry."

My smile was a tad more genuine thanks to the hit of caffeine. "I am too. It's not much fun finding out your entire marriage was a lie."

I waited anxiously to see if she'd take the bait. I

couldn't just dump everything on her, and I knew this wasn't the time to push for her story, but maybe if she saw there was some common ground between us, she'd feel safe letting me in.

I let out the breath I'd been holding as soon as she asked, "Do you want to talk about it?"

*Bingo.*

Her eyes widened as soon as the last word passed her lips, like she worried she was being nosey or something. "You don't have to, of course. It's your business. I just thought—"

"I found out shortly after my husband died that he'd been having an affair," I said, letting her off the hook with the truth. "That was bad enough, but I couldn't shake this feeling that I was missing something, so I went to a friend and asked him to do some digging. I found out yesterday that it hadn't just been an affair. He had a whole other family I never knew about. They had two kids together." I let out a bitter laugh, the pain from the day before having calcified into anger at some point. "It had been happening most of our marriage."

Ten years, to be precise, starting around the time I'd gotten pregnant with Avett.

"Oh, Blythe." She took a step closer to me, her brow furrowing as sadness filled her eyes. It was the first time she wasn't trying to hide herself away, and I couldn't help but notice how strikingly beautiful she was. "I don't know what to say. I'm so sorry."

"Thank you. It goes to show that things aren't always what they appear to be from the outside. I mean, we were married fifteen years. Together even longer. And he still turned out to be someone I don't even recognize. I guess there's no time limit on finding out the person you thought you knew best was something completely different."

She cast her eyes down. "No. I suppose there's not," she said quietly.

Deciding that I'd said enough, and silently hoping the seed I planted would take root, I headed for the exit, stopping beside her and placing my hand on her forearm. "Thanks for listening. Talking about it helps. Makes it feel like I'm not so alone." I gave her arm a gentle, comforting squeeze before I passed her on my way out. "I'll see you out there."

I caught Merritt's gaze more than once as the day progressed, noticing she was studying me in a way she hadn't before. A tiny niggling of hope bloomed that she might open up to me as well, and I might actually have a chance to help her.

Shortly before lunch the door opened, and I smiled my first real smile of the day as Sunny came waltzing in.

"Hey. This is a pleasant surprise." I raised my brows

playfully. "Wait. You don't have an appointment scheduled, do you?"

She sucked in a dramatic gasp, her eyes scanning over the artful pictures of pregnant women hanging on the walls of the waiting room. "Don't you dare put that devil on me."

Where I'd actually enjoyed being pregnant, it had been different for Sunny. She'd developed preeclampsia with her daughter, Brynne, that led to bed rest, and my best friend had never been one to lie around. Growing up, she'd always been busy. If there was something to get into, her name was written all over it. She'd been a cheerleader, not to mention student council president, and prom queen our senior year. She was always on the go, so bed rest had been her own personal form of torture. Poor Aaron had developed a nervous tic, having to put up with her. It had taken a few years and much bribing on her husband's part to talk her around to one more child. Fortunately, things had been a little easier with Cooper.

She made the sign of the cross then began waving her hands in front of her like she was trying to ward off bad vibes or negative energy. "Now I'm gonna have to sage myself when I get home."

I couldn't help but laugh at my friend's antics. It felt good to actually laugh after the day I had prior, and if there was anyone who could do that for me, it was Sunny. She could do a really good job of living up to her full name sometimes. She could be a ray of sunshine when she wanted to, but there was also a side of her she wouldn't hesitate to throw down for the ones she loved.

"What brings you by?"

She bent at the waist and rested her elbows on the counter between us. She blinked three times in rapid succession "No reason. I had a free day and thought I'd come by to see if you want to grab lunch."

I narrowed my eyes, knowing that blink was a precursor to a lie. "You just happened to have a free day, huh?" I asked suspiciously.

She let out an exasperated huff. "Okay, fine. I needed to see for myself that you're okay." The earlier humor disappeared, her eyes now swimming with concern. "Let me take you to lunch, B. We can hit Evergreen or Muffin Top. Your choice." She lowered her voice. "Just let me make sure you're okay. Please."

I nodded, my chest swelling a bit. It was only fair I give her that, seeing as I would have done the same exact thing if the shoe were on the other foot. I wasn't surprised that she knew. I trusted that Lincoln and Rhodes would remain professional and keep their word about not sharing, but this was a small town, and small towns—especially this one—fed on gossip. Things managed to slip through no matter how tightly you tried to keep the lid on. It felt good to be back where my support system was. Sunny had been there for me as best she could after Elliott died. She called regularly to check up on me and even flew to Indiana shortly after it happened, staying until after the funeral. Now, being in the same place meant the shoulders I had to lean on weren't temporary or over the phone.

"Okay. And I choose Muffin Top. The only way I'm making it through this day is if I can get a cup of coffee the size of my head."

BY THE TIME I finished relaying to her everything Lincoln had told me, Sunny's face was so red she could have stood at the intersection in the middle of downtown and acted as a stop sign. My best friend practically vibrated with rage as her fingers tore at the uneaten croissant on the plate in front of her, shredding it into teeny-tiny pieces.

"That mother*fucker*," she hissed, mindful to keep her voice low, seeing as Muffin Top was a family establishment. "If he were alive I'd castrate the cheating fuckhead. No, you know what? I'm stopping by the library on the way home. Maybe they have some books on witchcraft or something that'll teach us how to raise a person from the dead so I can cut his pecker off and kill him all over again."

I snorted up a bit of my coffee at her colorful threat. "Jeez, Sun . . . don't hold back or anything."

She leaned forward and dropped her voice to a menacing hiss. "That piece of shit was playing house with another woman!" she whisper-yelled before flopping back in her seat and raking a hand through her hair. "My God," she said on a sigh. "He might not have been my favorite person, but I never expected *this*."

That was a testament to how good of a friend Sunny was. From the first time they met, there had been an underlying tension between them. Elliott hadn't bothered to hide his animosity toward my best friend, and more than once we'd gotten into a fight over him acting like an entitled snob. But she'd never once said a negative word.

I should have seen that for the red flag it was, but what they said about hindsight really was true.

"You never told me why you didn't like him."

Her brows pulled together in a frown. "Of course I didn't. You're my best friend and he was your husband and the father of your kids. What kind of person would I have been if I talked shit about the man you chose to spend your life with? As long as he made you happy, that was all that mattered to me."

My heart clenched as I picked up my latte and took a sip. "Well, I think if there ever was a time for you to tell me how you really feel it would be now."

Her expression fell, sadness filling her gaze. "Honey, I don't think—"

"Please, Sun. I feel like I lived all these years with blinders on. You weren't the only person I sensed who didn't care for my husband, but no one ever said anything. Tell me now. I need to know."

She let out a heavy sigh. "He was a pretentious ass," she finally said, blurting the words like she was trying to get them out as quickly as possible. "He always acted like he was better than us whenever we came to visit, like being from a small town made us beneath him or something. He never came right out and said it, it was more like a feeling. He'd get these little digs in then act like it was all a joke. But I couldn't shake the feeling that he would have been happy if you dropped everyone from your old life."

I sniffled, her figure going blurry as my eyes welled up. I blinked the tears back, refusing to let them fall as I reached across the table and placed a hand over hers. "I'm so sorry he made you feel like that."

She flipped her hand over and wrapped her fingers

around mine, giving them a squeeze. "None of that mattered, B. He was arrogant, sure, but he was also a good father to those babies, and you were happy. You were so heartbroken after . . ." Her throat worked on a thick swallow. "After you and Rhodes broke up. I hated how sad you were all the time. You started smiling again when you met him. That was all I wanted for you."

"God, I missed you," I whispered. As bruised and battered as my heart was over the events of the past several months, I could feel pieces of it stitching back together, thanks to Sunny.

"I missed you too, B." She quirked her head and smiled. "You're my bestie for life. Things suck right now, but you're going to get through this. I'm here for you. Your family is here. We're going to make sure you get to the other side. I promise."

I couldn't have asked for a better friend than Sunny, and I didn't want to think about where I'd be if I didn't have her in my life.

"To be honest, I can't believe you aren't curled up in your bed right now. You're so dang strong, Blythe. If it were me, I would have lost it."

I let out a dry chuckle and rubbed at my temples. My crying jags had given me a headache that I hadn't been able to get rid of. "Oh, believe me, I lost it. And it wasn't pretty. After Lincoln . . ." I swallowed hard, trying to force down the ball of emotion making my throat tight. "I had to get out of there. I went to the lookout and screamed into the sky until my throat felt like it had been shredded by broken glass."

Her face fell and her fingers tensed around mine again. "Oh, honey."

I shook my head as I remembered how badly I'd broken down. "Rhodes was there. He witnessed the whole thing, but I'm too damn tired to be embarrassed about it."

"First, you have nothing to be embarrassed about," she said firmly, her tone brooking zero argument. "And second, I'm not surprised you ran into him there. He goes up to the lookout all the time."

My heart kicked up and my spine straightened. Sunny knew about Rhodes's and my spot because I'd told her about it, but she'd never been there herself, at least she hadn't before I moved away. "He does?"

She nodded. "He won't say it, but I think he goes there to feel close to you. It's been that way since he got back. If we can't find him it's because he's there. Sometimes he'll disappear for a couple days, camping out up there."

My mind raced back to what he said as he held me like I was made of glass and it was his job to protect me from anything that might break me. "He told me he still loves me," I confessed quietly. I waited a beat for Sunny to have some sort of reaction to that, but it never came. "Why don't you look surprised?"

She lifted her shoulders in a shrug and tossed a piece of shredded croissant into her mouth. "Because I'm not. I know my brother better than he knows himself. And even though I still want to kick his ass for hurting you, I know he ripped his heart out the day he broke up with you. I always respected your wishes not to bring him up, but there hasn't been anyone for him since you."

A bitter, unpleasant feeling rolled through me as I remembered back to the woman in the grocery store. I couldn't stop the scoff that burst past my lips. "Yeah, I don't buy that."

"I'm not saying he's been a saint. What I mean is that not a single one of them has been important. In twenty years, he hasn't brought a single one of them around to meet us."

The bite of Danish I'd just taken lodged in my throat. There was no one more important to Rhodes than his family, so the fact that he hadn't brought a single woman around any of them spoke volumes.

I didn't know what to think about that. All I knew was I wasn't prepared for how that knowledge made me feel.

# Chapter Thirteen

## Blythe

You know the old saying: when it rains, it pours? I could personally attest to how true that was thanks to the past two weeks. It all started with Ainsley bringing home a nasty stomach virus that moved through the house at a rapid pace, leaving only myself behind. If I thought my kids were bad when they were sick, it was nothing compared to my six-foot-two, two-hundred-plus-pounds-of-muscle brother.

Turned out, his dog came by his pathetic personality honestly, because Tristan had been the worst patient out of all four of them. It was really sad when a thirty-six-year-old man was a worse patient than a barfing four-year-old.

The only reason I hadn't smothered my brother with

a pillow then called my mom and Sunny over to help me bury his dead body in the woods was because the bug only lasted twenty-four hours. Twenty-five and Tristan would have mysteriously disappeared, and I was confident I'd watched enough true crime shows and listened to enough podcasts to get away with it. If not, I could've always played up to the sympathy of the women on the jury. Surely, they would have understood that men were whiny little bitches when they got sick.

I was so glad I managed to stay healthy, because after a week of puke, fevers, and other bodily fluids, I didn't have it in me to also take care of myself, and, Lord knew, there was no one else who would have done it had I fallen prey.

Just when I'd been ready to believe the worst had passed, two nights ago Avett shouted from the upstairs shower, "Mom! The water's doin' something funny," right before a pipe in the kitchen burst. Of course, Tristan hadn't been home at the time and wasn't answering his phone, so it had taken twice as long for me to find the water shut-off for the house than it should have.

With no water and the plumber claiming it wasn't going to be a quick fix, the kids and I had to pack what little we had that wasn't still in storage and relocate to my parents' place, a problem in itself.

After the four of us had moved out, my mom and Trick had decided to downsize, moving into a two-bedroom, two-bath on the outskirts of town. At present, the four of us were all sharing a bathroom, and I was sleeping on the sofa while my three kids were crammed into the guest room. That had managed to shine a glaring light on the fact that I hadn't done a very good job of finding something permanent for my kids. They needed permanence and security, but so far, all I'd given them were temporary stopovers while I struggled to get my shit together.

They deserved better. Unfortunately, between sickness and the day it took to dry the flooded kitchen, I had managed to burn through most of my time off from work, so finding the time to look for a place that would work for my family was harder than I expected.

I kept waiting for a break, for things to start getting easier—or at least even out—but it felt like every time I was about to get my feet under me, the rug was pulled out all over again.

That was why, when Sunny insisted that I needed a night out—no kids, no responsibilities—I hadn't put up a fight. I couldn't remember the last time I'd dressed up and spent a night on the town with friends. It had been hard to find time in Indiana. Elliott was always working —or so I thought—and his family wasn't very big on babysitting. Not that I had many friends I could go out with anyway. My life there basically consisted of my husband and children. I hadn't minded. I loved taking care of my family, but being back in Hope Valley where I had a built-in circle of friends, it was easy to see what I had been missing.

I lifted my pint glass to my lips and drank back the cold, crisp amber liquid, letting it coat my tongue before swallowing it. A lot had changed about The Tap Room while I was away. Rory and Cord's daughter, Lennix, had taken over running it, and turned it from just a bar into an actual brewery, complete with an in-house brewmaster and everything. They hosted tastings and tours, and even had a gorgeous event space to rent for weddings or parties.

But other things about it had stayed the same, such as the amazing selection of beer they served. Not that I'd had a chance to sample what they had to offer before I moved away—at least as far as my parents knew.

Lennix had barely been a toddler when I moved away, but I was getting to know her as a woman tonight and see all the qualities she shared with her mother. Getting to know her, I couldn't help but feel sorry for her father, because I had a sneaking suspicion she'd been more than a handful growing up. There was too much of Rory's wild in her to ever be tamed.

"This place is fantastic," I told her as she dropped off a second round for me, Sunny, Sunny's sister, Holly, and Lennix's sister-in-law, Rae. Rae's parents were also close friends with mine, but they'd moved away, only coming back to town for short visits, so I hadn't gotten a chance to know her until now. It wasn't hard to see why Zach had fallen for the former big-city transplant.

I scanned the bar, taking in the rustic vibe of the raw wood features, the high beams, and the large glass windows. Lennix had somehow managed to build everything out while still keeping all the charm that had made this place a favorite spot for decades.

"It feels like the same bar, only . . . more. If that makes any sense."

She beamed with pride at my attempt to compliment her. "It does. I get what you're trying to say, and I really appreciate it. My grandparents and Mom were scared when I first came to them with the idea of expanding. They were worried we would ruin the history of this place."

"You didn't," I assured her. "You just added to it."

Rae lifted her drink in the air in salute. "And we get to reap the benefits of Len's brilliance with free drinks for life."

I laughed as Holly and Sunny cheered.

"Not on your life, cheapskate," Lennix threw back.

"You forget we're family? I know you're loaded. First round was on the house because I love you crazy assholes, but you're paying for the rest. This is a business, not a charity."

My head fell back on a deep belly laugh. I couldn't remember the last time I'd laughed so freely. Hell, I couldn't remember the last time I had fun like this. In the past few hours, I hadn't thought about all the ways my life had been turned upside down. I hadn't remembered to be sad or angry or stressed. I'd been able to push aside the fact that the first boy I had ever loved had been invading nearly every single one of my thoughts for the past two weeks. That I couldn't stop thinking about him, so I'd taken the coward's way out and was avoiding him like the plague because everything he was making me feel was so damn complicated.

I'd simply been present in the moment with an amazing group of women who were determined to show me a good time.

I'd been away for so long that there were a bunch of new faces in the bar, but there were also plenty of old ones as well. And one of those old faces wasn't a particularly welcome sight as he moved in my direction. I had to swallow the groan that wanted to escape my chest.

"Shit," Sunny hissed from beside me, her eyes landing on the figure pushing through the crowd and growing closer. "Looks like you've pinged on Lonny Oswald's radar."

"Looks like it," I grumbled, bracing for the interaction that was about to happen. Lonny Oswald had been an asshole back in middle school and high school, and judging from the smarmy grin on his face, he hadn't managed to change his ways since then.

He was the stereotypical jock who thought his shit didn't stink because he knew how to throw a football. He and Rhodes had been in the same grade all through school, and for some reason, Lonny got off on giving Rhodes shit whenever possible. I always suspected it was jealousy, because he knew he'd never be half as talented or smart as the kid he looked down on just because Rhodes hadn't grown up with the same privileges as he had. But it hadn't mattered how much money Lonny's parents had, it was never enough to buy the shithead a lick of class or sense.

When Rhodes and I started dating, he'd actually tried getting to him through me. He tried flirting and making passes whenever he thought Rhodes might see, doing everything in his power to goad him into a fight.

His attempt at swagger was severely diminished, thanks to the beer gut hanging over the waistband of his jeans.

He stopped on my side of the table, only a few feet

separating us. "Well, well, well, look who the cat dragged in." He licked his lips as he looked me up and down, and I didn't bother to hide my cringe. "Still lookin' as good as always, Blythe."

"Lonny," I said flatly, taking another sip of my beer.

"How 'bout you and me go for a spin around the dance floor?"

"No thanks," I answered, hoping that would be enough to move him along. Unfortunately, he was still as bad at taking a hint as he had been back when we were growing up.

He drew closer, leaning his elbow on the high-top table beside my pint glass and caging me in with his body. "Aw, come on, sexy. Don't be like that. We can have a good time together."

"Jesus, Oswald," Sunny clipped, her top lip curled up in disgust. "Get a clue. She's not interested."

He turned to bare his yellowed teeth at my best friend. "No one asked you, trailer trash."

My back shot straight and my eyes narrowed on the man standing too close to me. "Since you won't listen to her, maybe you'll listen to me," I said, my voice growing scarily low in the way that always brought my kids to attention. "I tried letting you down nicely so you could walk away with your pride intact, but you just insulted my best friend and if there's one thing I won't tolerate, it's someone insulting the people I care about. So now I'm going to humiliate you. No, Lonny, I do not want to dance with you. In fact, I'd rather have a rubbing alcohol enema than have your hands anywhere near my body."

"Oh my God," Rae breathed out from the other side of the table, her wide eyes pinned on me.

I didn't miss the way Sunny grinned or that the conversations around us had gone quiet and more and more people were turning their attention our way, but I was on a roll.

"The fact that you think you have the right to call someone else trailer trash when you're standing here looking like a reject roadie for a ZZ Top cover band is downright laughable. But what's even funnier is that you actually came over here thinking you had a shot in hell with me. You obviously took one too many hits to the head in high school, so I'm going to spell it out for you so you can't possibly misunderstand. There isn't a universe in which a man like you could *ever* land a woman like me. You're swinging way above your weight class, buddy. It's time for you to move along."

Snickers sounded from all around us, but the women at my table didn't bother trying to cover up their laughter. They let it fly, right in the prick's face.

Halfway through my diatribe, Lonny's face started to grow red with embarrassment, but by the time I finished, he was an unhealthy shade of purple. "You think you're hot shit," he seethed, venom coating his tone.

I took a slow, casual drink. "Nope." I made sure to pop the P obnoxiously. "I know I am. Now run along before you do something to really piss me off."

"Fuckin' bitch," he hissed, shoving away from our table hard enough to make the glasses rattle, but I didn't so much as flinch, refusing to give him any kind of reaction.

"What the fuck did you just call her?"

My blood went cold and my back shot straight. I knew who that voice belonged to, and more specifically, I knew that tone. It meant shit was about to hit the fan.

Sure enough, when I looked back over my shoulder, Rhodes was standing there, and he was staring at Lonny like he was about to rip the man limb from limb with his bare hands.

# Chapter Fourteen

## Rhodes

It had been two weeks since my run-in with Blythe at the lookout. Two weeks since I held her as she cried. Since I nearly kissed her. Two miserable weeks of not seeing her, and I was going out of my goddamn skin.

I wasn't too proud to admit the reason I was currently bellied up to the bar at The Tap Room was because I managed to overhear a conversation my sisters were having about a night out on the town. Blythe's name was mentioned and that sealed the deal for me.

My buddy, Hardin, cleared his throat, drawing my attention away from the table I'd been watching for the past hour.

"You know, not to sound all needy and shit, but when you invited me out for a beer, I thought *maybe* there'd be a bit of conversation. Maybe a game of pool or darts. At the very least, I expected you to ask me how I've been since the divorce. What I didn't expect was to sit here and be ignored all damn night so you could creep on your ex from across the bar."

A chuckle rattled up my chest. "I'm sorry, puddin'. Are you feelin' neglected?"

Hardin sucked in his cheeks and clicked his tongue. "Yes. But you cover the next round and I'll consider forgiving you."

"That I can do." I raised two fingers to catch the bartender's attention and pointed to Hardin's empty rocks glass and my pint, silently requesting a refill.

"You know, you could have just told me why we were really comin' here tonight. It's not like I wouldn't get it. It's been Blythe for you since you were seventeen."

I'd known Hardin most of my life, both of us having been born and raised in Hope Valley, but it wasn't until Marco came into the picture that I'd gotten to know him better. Marco and Hardin's dad were friends, and Marco's friends quickly became family friends. Everyone in his and Gypsy's circle had taken us in, and we'd gone from being a group of misfits to having a support system bigger than I ever would have expected.

Hardin and I had been closest in age of all the kids, so it came naturally that we'd grown tight. He knew when Blythe and I started dating. He was my sounding board as my first deployment grew closer and I started to get in my own head about not being good enough. He'd tried his best to knock some sense into me, insisting that Blythe wasn't going to realize she could do better once I was gone, and that ending our relationship would be a mistake, not that I listened. He was also the one who used his fake ID to buy a case of beer one town over so I could get trashed after ignoring his advice and breaking up with her anyway. And not once had he said "I told you so."

That friendship had lasted through my time in the Army and his stint in veterinary school until we both eventually made our way back here.

I stood with him at his wedding. Hell, I was godfather to his oldest daughter. And I'd returned the favor, taking him out to get him shit-faced when his divorce was finalized.

"You know, she looks a lot better than she did when she first got back to town."

"She does," I said gruffly, emotion lodging in my throat.

My gaze shifted back across the bar, homing in on her in an instant. He wasn't wrong. When she first arrived back in town, she looked more like a ghost than a person, a shell of who she had once been. Now the color had returned to her cheeks, her hair regained its luster, and she was finally starting to put on some of the weight she'd lost. Sadness and anger still lingered in her ocean eyes, but they weren't as flat and dull as they had been. Little by little, the Blythe I had known was resurfacing.

The bartender came over and set our new round in front of us before smiling up at Hardin through the fan of her lashes. He shot her a wink that made her blush before picking up the glass and murmuring, "Thanks, gorgeous."

"Christ, man." I let out a grunted laugh and shook my head as the woman behind the bar moved down to take care of the line of customers, glancing back over her shoulder every few seconds. "Anyone ever told you not to shit where you eat?"

My buddy had kind of gone off the rails after his divorce and started whoring around town.

"Nothin' wrong with a little harmless flirting."

"I agree, but is that really all you're doin' right now? Look, brother, I'm not sayin' you should become a monk or anything, maybe just practice a little more discretion. Have your fun over in Hidalgo Grapevine where it's less likely to blow back on you. You're the only vet in town, Hard. You really want to walk into work one day and see a waiting room full of one-night stands?"

He let out a scoffing laugh. "Nothing bad's happened so far."

I shook my head. "I can guarantee that woman right there"—I pointed at the bartender still making eyes at him—"is less than six degrees separated. Your stepmom owns the most popular coffee shop in town. You really think she doesn't know that chick? It's a small town, and people talk. You want to run the risk of your girls hearing somethin' they shouldn't?"

I knew I had him when I mentioned his daughters. I wasn't sure there was a better father on the planet than Hardin Drake. There wasn't a thing he wouldn't do for his girls. That included sitting through an hour-long torture session where they slathered his face with makeup and glitter, painted his nails bright pink, and stuck tiny little flower clips all through his hair. He wore that shit with pride because it made them happy.

"All right, I see your point. I'll be more careful."

I clapped him on the shoulder and took a pull of my beer.

"Speakin' of gossip," he started, turning the tables around on me, "you know the whole town's talkin', right?"

I looked in his direction, my brow furrowed. "About what?"

He let out a sigh and reached around to rub the back

of his neck, discomfort spreading across his face. "Word got out that Blythe's husband turned out to be a piece of shit before he died." My mouth pulled in a hard line, the muscle in my jaw ticking. Hardin lifted his hands in surrender. "Hey, man. I'm just the messenger here. You know discretion doesn't exist in a place like this. You can try to keep things under wraps, but word's gonna get out, no matter what."

I spun back to face the line of taps on the back wall, bracing my forearms on the bar top. "I get that. I just don't want people talkin' shit behind her back. She's been through enough."

He turned to face me head-on, his expression clean of the earlier humor. "They aren't talking shit, brother. They're talking about the two of you."

It felt like someone had shoved their fist into my chest and was squeezing my heart. "What are they saying?"

The prick slowly lifted his glass to his lips and sipped on his bourbon neat like he had all the time in the goddamn world. "Well, the general consensus is that people want the two of you back together."

I'd barely had time to wrap my mind around that statement when a voice spoke up from behind me. "Hey, Rhodes. I thought that was you over here."

*Fucking hell.*

I schooled my expression and twisted my stool around. "Grace," I greeted with a tilt of my lips so miniscule it could barely be considered a smile.

She was dressed in painted-on jeans and a shirt that showed more than a decent amount of cleavage. She batted her eyes much like the way the bartender had done to Hardin a few minutes ago and cocked out her hip. "It's really good to see you," she said brightly.

"Yeah, you too," I said, mainly because I didn't have a clue what else to say, but I knew it was a mistake as soon her face lit up.

The song the band was playing came to an end and they moved right into a slower number. "Oh, I love this song!" she declared enthusiastically. "It would be a shame not to dance to it. Feel like taking me around the dance floor?"

My head spun with ways I could shoot her down politely, but as soon as I opened my mouth to speak, I caught sight of something that set my blood to a rolling boil in an instant.

"Mother*fucker*," I hissed as I shot to my feet. "You've got to be shittin' me."

The seductive look she'd been shooting me fell off her face at my sudden anger. "Is everything okay?"

"Sorry, Grace. You'll have to excuse me." I pushed past her before I finished speaking, barely hearing her muttered, "Uh, y-yeah. Sure. I'll catch up with you later," as I started toward the other end of the bar.

I didn't know what the fuck that son of a bitch, Lonny Oswald, was saying to her, but it was clear from the narrow-eyed glare she was shooting his way that whatever it was had pissed her off, and as her mouth moved, I could see his face growing redder and redder.

My girl always had a gift when it came to flaying a person open with her sharp tongue, and from the looks of it, she was currently slicing that stupid bastard up one side and down the other. Only problem was, Lonny Oswald had always been an asshole, but as he got older, he'd gotten even worse.

"Fuckin' bitch," I heard him throw in her face as I closed in on Blythe's table, and I instantly saw red.

My molars ground together and my hands clenched into fists. "What the fuck did you just call her?"

I'd had a hair-trigger temper when I was younger, but the Army had done a good job of working that out of me as it taught me how to become the man I wanted to be. Gypsy and Marco might have started those lessons by teaching me what it meant to be a good man, but my time in the service finished those lessons and taught me how to get there.

I hadn't been quick to anger in a really long time, but all it took was one asshole looking at Blythe in a way that didn't sit well with me to set me off. When it came to her, I would never hesitate to act first. It was in my blood to protect her, a sense that ran so deep it was etched into my bones.

Oswald smiled his slick, oily smile. "Well look who's come runnin' to save the day. White Trash Soldier Boy. Should've known you wouldn't be too far from where she was. Always chasin' after her like a pathetic, flea-riddled mutt that got kicked in the head one too many times."

My smile felt as vicious as I was sure it looked. "You always had a mouth on you. Maybe I should do this town a favor and break your jaw so nobody had to hear you talk for a while."

Blythe pushed out of her seat, standing up and coming beside me to place her hand on my arm. "Rhodes, don't."

"Yeah, Rhodes. Listen to your little slut."

I lunged, but before I could get close enough, Hardin was there, pushing me back and keeping me from breaking every bone in that fucker's face.

I could just make out Blythe's voice through the red haze of rage clouding my head. "Rhodes, please. He's not worth it."

"Yeah, why don't you get outta here, Trashbury," he mocked, using the sorry excuse of an insult he'd made out of my last name back in middle school. "Run back home to your stripper whore sister and all those other white trash brothers and sisters of yours where you belong."

There wouldn't have been time for me to react if I'd wanted to. One second Blythe was right beside me and the next she was standing between me and Oswald, with the latter collapsing to the ground, gasping for breath and clutching at his throat where she'd just punched him. One hit and my girl had dropped that fucker like a sack of rocks.

"Holy shit," Lennix cried out. "I have the biggest girl crush right now."

I moved fast, grabbing her around the waist and hoisting her off her feet when she stepped up like she was preparing to kick him while he was down. "What did I say about insulting the people I care about, huh?" she shouted at the waste of space on the floor as he continued to choke.

"Jesus," I grunted as she struggled against me. I held tight as I started moving us toward the exit. "Easy, killer. You've done enough damage. Let's get you home before you get yourself arrested."

"Wait. I came with Sunny."

"I'll call you in the morning," my sister called out,

waving a hand over her head with a big, shit-eating grin on her face. "Love you!"

The fight went out of Blythe as I carried her through the door and outside, her hands resting on my forearms wrapped around her stomach and her feet dangling in the air. "You know I can walk, right?"

Oh, I was well aware. I just wasn't sure when I would get another chance like this—or if I'd get one at all—so I was determined to make the most of it. I took her as far as my truck before placing her back on her feet, beeping the locks, and opening the passenger door for her.

She stood in the open doorway of the truck, trepidation flashed in her Caribbean eyes as she looked around the dark, quiet parking lot. "You really don't need to do this. Sunny can take me home."

I lifted my hand and braced it on the edge of the door, blocking any path she might use to escape. "Get in the truck, Angel. I'm takin' you back to your brother's."

Her eyes narrowed into unhappy slits for a few seconds before she let out a huff, grumbling, "Whatever," when she realized I wasn't going to move or back down.

I waited for her to buckle the seatbelt over her lap before shutting the door and rounding the hood. I used those few short seconds to try to get my shit together. My heart had started racing as soon as I saw Oswald in Blythe's space, and it hadn't stopped yet. To make matters worse, watching her take that shithead to the ground had caused my dick to take notice.

There was something about her vehement defense of me and my family that heated my blood. That side of her had always turned me on—her steadfast protectiveness.

I inhaled deeply, pulling the crisp, pine-scented night air into my lungs and letting it soothe me as I pulled open the driver's side door and climbed in.

"Actually, would you mind taking me to my parents' place?" she asked as I pushed the button to start the engine. "The kids and I are staying there for the time being."

My brows dipped together in the center as I turned to her. "Isn't their place kind of small for all four of you?"

She made a scoffing sound and tilted her head back against the headrest. "That's an understatement. It isn't ideal, but it's the only choice I have at the moment. A pipe burst at Tristan's and flooded the kitchen." She let out a sigh that denoted her exhaustion. "It's a mess." Her voice lowered a few more octaves as she said, "Everything's such a mess."

I would have given anything to fix things for her, but if there was anything I'd learned from having sisters, it was that sometimes women needed to vent without having the answers thrown at them.

I placed my hand on the seat behind Blythe and twisted to look out the back window as I reversed out of the spot with my mind reeling.

Silence filled the cab of my truck, along with the smell of her intoxicating perfume. It was the same as it had been all those years ago. Like amber and roses. Despite how subtle the fragrance was, it packed the strongest punch.

"How's the hand, slugger?"

She lifted the hand she'd used to punch Oswald in the throat and flexed it, opening and closing her fingers. "A little sore, but nothing a little ice won't fix." A pleased smile pulled at her mouth. "I'd be lying if I said it hadn't felt really freaking good to do that."

My dick jerked against my thigh like the fucking thing was trying to punch out of my jeans. Still, despite my arousal, I couldn't shake the concern I felt tightening my chest. "You need to be careful with guys like Lonny Oswald, Blythe."

She waved that away. "Oh, it's fine. Besides, that prick's deserved a punch in the throat since we were kids."

"Can't deny that. Just . . . try to stay away from him,

okay?" Something told me she'd put herself on that asshole's radar, and I hated the thought of her being there.

# Chapter Fifteen

## Blythe

Gretchen came speed-skipping into the break room with Diana and Merritt close on her heels. I swirled the wooden stirrer around in my mug as I turned from the coffeemaker. Gretchen and Diana had grins a mile wide while Merritt looked more curious and unsure than anything.

I frowned at them before hitching my brows up as I took a sip of my coffee. "What's happening right now? You guys are being weird."

Gretchen did a little hop and clasped her hands in front of her. "There's someone here to see you."

My head tilted to the side in confusion. "To see me? Who?"

"I don't know. I didn't ask his name."

Diana chimed in then. "She was struck dick-stupid and forgot to ask."

I choked on the sip I'd just taken. "*What?*" I croaked.

Gretchen fanned her face and rolled her eyes back in her head. "Can you blame me? The dude is *gorgeous*."

I could only think of one man who was worthy of that kind of salivating. An entire horde of butterflies came to life in my belly as my fingers gripped my mug tighter. It had been two days since Rhodes had given me a ride home from the bar, and I hadn't been able to stop thinking about him. Because my life wasn't complicated enough, I had to go and start fixating on my ex again.

"Um, okay . . . thanks." I started out of the break room, the three of them plastering themselves against the wall so I could pass, then skittering after me.

I bypassed the entry for the nook where our desks were, and moved straight into the waiting room. Sure enough, Rhodes was standing there, his back to me, as he took in the pictures lining the wall. It was impossible not to notice the way his jeans molded to his firm, round behind, or the way the muscles on his back danced with each inhale beneath the material of his shirt. Rhodes had always had a big presence, but it was so much *more* now, almost overwhelming.

I cleared my throat to get his attention, not trusting that my voice wouldn't come out as a squeak.

He turned around, a grin already firmly in place, and damn if it wasn't a flutter-inducing one. "Hey, Angel."

Diana squeaked and Gretchen let out dreamy sigh at the use of the pet name Rhodes had given me when we were kids. Growing up, it had been impossible *not* to notice my best friend's older brother, and I would have been lying if I said I hadn't formed a crush long before he ever noticed me. And having him call me *Angel* only made that crush stronger. *Angel* was what got me through when I thought I would never have a chance in hell, and *Angel* was what had solidified my love for him.

That was why hearing it the night he'd come over for dinner had hurt so damn much. I hadn't been able to handle it. It was still hard. But I would have been lying if I said it wasn't starting to feel good.

"Hey. What are you doing here?"

His gaze darted over my shoulder, and I turned to see that Heather, and even Dr. Shaundry, had joined the huddle behind the desk to listen in.

"Any chance you can take a break? It'll be short. I don't want to take up too much of your time."

"Um . . ." I looked back at the girls again and bugged my eyes out, silently communicating that they were all being ridiculous. "Yeah, sure. Follow me."

The thick soles of his motorcycle boots thumped against the floor behind me as I led him back to the break room. "Can I get you a cup of coffee or anything?" I offered, pointing at the snazzy machine I'd come to love like it was my fourth child.

"No, thanks." He tucked his hands into the pockets of his jeans. I wasn't sure if it was intentional or not, but the action stretched the faded denim at his front and accentuated his bulge, not that it needed accentuating. "Like I said," he continued, bursting the bubble of lust that was suddenly filling my head, "I'll make this fast. I've been thinking about your dilemma, and I think I might have a solution."

I crossed my arms over my chest and raised my brows in curiosity. "I wasn't aware I had a dilemma."

His lips curved, the white of his straight teeth standing out against the dark scruff coating his jaw. Humor danced in his amber eyes like he enjoyed going back and forth with me. "Your living situation."

Oh, *that* dilemma.

"Rhodes, I've been looking online for days without any luck. Unless you've magically discovered a place that's available now and is big enough for my kids to have their own rooms so they don't have to stay cramped up on top of each other, I don't see how you have a solution."

His grin spread even wider, and I knew that, beneath that stubble, there was a place on his left cheek that pressed deeper but not quite deep enough to be called a dimple. "Well, it so happens that I know just the place."

"Are you serious?" My eyes rounded and my arms fell. I took a step toward him, my excitement building that my kids and I might finally have a place to stay that we fit in. A place that was permanent and not just another stopover. "Where?"

"Right outside of town. You have time durin' your lunch break, I'm happy to show you."

"Yeah. Yes! I have time." I bounced on the balls of my feet. "Oh my God. This is amazing. Thank you so much."

Before I could stop myself, I threw my arms around his neck to hug him, only realizing what I'd done when his arms came up instantly and wrapped around my waist. His woodsy, spicy cologne tickled my nose as I breathed in, and as nice as it felt to be held, I knew staying the way we were any longer would be dangerous.

His arms fell away as I lowered to flat feet and took a step back. "So . . . should I meet you there?"

"I'll come back and pick you up. What time do you go to lunch?"

I really wasn't sure if getting in a car with him again was a smart move. "Rhodes, you don't have to—"

He cut me off and repeated, "I'll come back and pick you up."

I propped my hands on my hips and let out a quiet chuckle. "God. How did I manage to forget how stubborn you could be?"

"I don't know." His tone was a low rumble that I felt in my chest. "Because I never forgot a single thing about you."

MY MOUTH FELL open as soon as the trees that lined the short drive opened up and the house came into view.

"Rhodes," I breathed. It was beautiful. And big. And there was no way in hell I was going to be able to afford a place like this unless I was willing to dip into the college savings I'd set up for the kids with Elliott's life insurance. Which I wasn't going to do.

He shot me a quick grin before facing forward and guiding the truck over the gravel drive and stopping near the steps leading to the porch that wrapped around the entire first floor. "What do you think?"

I released a choking laugh, shaking my head in bewilderment. "I think . . . it's going to be *way* out of my price range. Rhodes, there's no way I can afford this place."

He shifted into park, hitting the ignition button and killing the engine. "I think you'll be surprised. Come on. Let's go check it out."

The hope that had sprung to life earlier started to shrivel as I climbed the porch steps and waited for Rhodes to open the front door. I should have told him not to bother showing me around, because I knew from looking at the outside, I was going to fall in love with the place, and the disappointment would sting like hell when I had to walk away from it.

I didn't know how he knew about this place, but I was shocked that a house like this hadn't been snapped up right away.

He pushed the door open, and a second later the entryway filled with the sharp sound of rapid clicking before a big dog came skidding around the corner, it's nails scrabbling on the wood floors.

"Whoa." I took a step back, intimidated by the dog's size despite the tongue lolling out the side of its mouth.

"Koda, calm," Rhodes ordered in a firm tone. Almost instantly, the dog skidded to a stop, her rear end wiggling like crazy with the force of her wagging tail. "Don't be scared. She's sweet as can be. She just looks scary."

I held out my hand for her to sniff, smiling when she

butted it with her head, demanding to be petted. "What is she? I'm not sure I've ever seen this breed before."

"She's a Belgian Tervuren."

I stroked down her black muzzle before scratching behind her ears, the rest of her silky coat a shiny fawn color. "She's beautiful. But who does she belong to?"

"We can get to that later. Come on." He grabbed my hand and started pulling me deeper into the house. "You're gonna love this kitchen."

He wasn't wrong. The huge kitchen called to my stress-cooker's heart, that was for sure, but as much as the stainless steel appliances and six-burner Z-Line were calling to me, I was more concerned about the fact that the open concept living, dining, and kitchen, were all fully furnished . . . and not in a staging kind of way, but in a someone-is-currently-living-here kind of way.

"Rhodes, wait." I pulled back on his hand, forcing him to stop and look back at me. "We can't just wander around. Somebody clearly lives here."

"It's fine, I promise."

He tugged my hand again, but I dug my heels in. "It's not. This is trespassing." I scanned the large, open space, ignoring the way my heart thumped at the thick forest that surrounded the property outside the massive wall of windows. But before I could fully appreciate the tranquil view, my attention caught on the picture frames that lined the raw wood mantel above the fireplace.

I recognized Rhodes's family in the photographs. Gypsy and Marco's wedding picture. Sunny's kids in different stages of growth. All of the siblings huddled together. Then, at the end, there was a photograph of a group of men standing in what looked to be a desert, dressed in combat uniform. And just to the right of center, with his arms thrown around the shoulders of the men on either side of him, was Rhodes, smiling for the camera.

I turned slowly to face him, unable to miss the sheepish look on his face. "Okay, just hear me out."

"This is your house?"

"Yes, but—"

I threw my arms out at my sides. "Why would you bring me here when it's *your* house? You knew I'd fall in love with this place," I threw out accusatorily.

"I did. And that's exactly why I brought you here." He brought his hands up in surrender when my face pinched up in annoyance. "Blythe, I want you and your kids to live here."

"With you?" My voice rose to a squeak on the last word.

"Yes."

My head fell back on a laugh. "Rhodes, that's insane. We can't live here."

"Why not?"

My smile fell and my expression turned deadpan. "You're kidding, right?"

Rhodes held his arms out, indicating the huge, open space all around him. "Think about it. It's the perfect solution. Koda's great with kids and having them around will be good for her. She's got a lot of energy and not a lot to do with it. They'd give her somewhere to focus it."

"I don't know—"

"And I have all this space," he added quickly before I could turn him down flat. "There's literally no one but me to use it. You and the kids will have your own rooms. You'll even have your own bathroom." I couldn't lie, that reason alone was almost enough to sway me. "And the best part is, it's totally free."

"Rhodes," I whispered, my face going soft. "I don't think this is a good idea."

"I'll stay out of your hair. You probably won't even notice I'm around."

"I come with a lot of baggage. Trust me, you don't want to have to deal with that. You have no idea how much I appreciate you offering this, but I need to think about my family. Every home we've lived in since we got here has been temporary. I mean, most of our stuff is still in storage, for crying out loud. It's not fair to keep moving them from place to place. I need to find somewhere permanent, somewhere that can actually be a home."

"That can be here," he insisted, taking a step closer to me. "Look, I understand your hesitation, but I don't have an ulterior motive here. I just want to help. Your kids are great, and I want them to have room to spread out. And I would be lying if I said it didn't get lonely here. You guys moving in would be helping me out just as much. I want you to be able to think of this as your home for as long as you want. Please, just . . . consider it. You guys deserve a fucking break. *You* deserve a break, Angel. Let this be that."

He spent a few more minutes showing me the rooms he thought we'd all like, and I knew my kids would love the ones he'd chosen. The free-standing tub in the bathroom he'd designated for me almost took me to my knees.

He didn't say another word about it as he drove me back to work, but as soon as he parked outside the building, he twisted in his seat to look at me. "Promise me you'll think about it, okay? There's no time limit on the offer."

I nodded, giving him a smile and thanking him for everything before climbing out of his truck. I wasn't sure I'd be able to think about anything else.

# Chapter Sixteen

## Blythe

"**W**hoa!" Avett exclaimed as he threw the door open and jumped out of the car. "Check this place out. It's huge!"

Adeline blinked, unbuckling her seatbelt and leaning between the front seats to stare out the windshield. "It's really pretty," she said in quiet awe, her reaction much more subdued than her older brother's but no less excited.

"It is. And wait until you see the inside."

She turned to look at me. "And I really get my own room?"

I smiled and reached up to tuck a lock of hair behind her ear before caressing her cheek. My little thinker liked to have her own space, and there hadn't been much of that in recent months. Having her own room would be a huge relief to her. "Yes, baby. You each have your own room."

"You think he gots horses?" Ainsley practically shouted, bouncing up and down in her booster like she's had pure sugar for breakfast.

"No, chickadee. No horses. But he does have a dog."

It was a wonder her excited squeal didn't shatter all the windows or burst my eardrums. "Lemme out! Lemme out! I wanna see!"

I didn't make her wait any longer. Climbing out of the car, I moved to the back door and threw it open, helping Ainsley out of her seat so she and Adeline could climb out and explore like their brother.

"Don't wander," I called out as I moved around the car and opened the back hatch. "And stay where I can see you!"

"Yes, ma'am," Adeline returned, taking her little sister's hand as they jog-skipped toward the house for further investigation.

The sound of tires crunching on gravel caught my attention, and I spun around to see the line of vehicles coming down the drive. Rhodes's truck was in the front, followed by Tristan's. Behind him, Trick steered his Suburban while my mom sat in the passenger seat, with Sunny and her family bringing up the rear in a white sedan. It was moving day, and it looked like my crew had finally arrived.

Rhodes slammed the door to his truck and started toward me. The top half of his face was hidden by the shadow his baseball cap cast, but I could see the wide grin stretching his lips clear as day. I shouldn't have taken notice of the way the sleeves of his white T-shirt bunched up above the swell of his biceps, like they couldn't stretch over the muscles, but I did.

"Hey, Angel," he greeted, stopping two feet in front of me and reaching up to twist his hat backward. *Damn it.* What was it about a backward ball cap that was so damn sexy? "Between Tris and me, we managed to get everything you had in storage packed up."

I dragged my tongue across my dry lips, preparing to thank him, when Ainsley's voice filled the air. "Mommy! I hear the dog!" Rhodes and I both turned in the direction of the front porch. My girls were standing at the door, their hands and ears pressed hard against the wood. "She's sayin' she wants to meet me!"

Rhodes let out a chuckle and started toward my daughters. "Is that what Koda's sayin'?"

Ainsley nodded earnestly, her turquois eyes big. "Uh-huh. She's so sad, bein' locked in there all by herself."

He smiled at my youngest with such tenderness and

affection I felt it in my chest. "Then we shouldn't keep her waitin'."

My girls bounced in place, waiting to meet the dog of the house.

He pressed the code to the lock—one he'd already given me, along with the key for backup—but before he opened the door, he said, "Now, she's a big girl, and she might look a little scary, but I promise she's gentle as a kitten. She'd never hurt you. But watch out for her tail when it really gets goin'. It can pack a punch if she whacks you with it."

My girls nodded, Adeline giving him a, "Yes, sir."

Sure enough, as soon as he pushed the door open, the dog I met at the beginning of the week charged out, her rear end swinging wildly. Her claws clicked against the wooden planks of the porch as her paws scrabbled around like she was dancing.

Ainsley let out an ear-piercing shriek. "*Eeeeeee*! She's so pretty!"

"Koda, calm," Rhodes ordered, and just like last time, the dog did her best to rein in her enthusiasm. She stood in place, her whole body practically vibrating as my kids loved all over her.

Avett came over just then, abandoning his attempt to climb one of the trees that lined the driveway. "That dog looks so much cooler than Uncle Tristan's!" he exclaimed before running up the steps to get in on the petting action.

"Christ," my brother grunted as he came up beside me, crossing his arms over his chest. "How quickly they're willin' to toss a guy over for one with a bigger dog."

I bumped my arm into his and laid my head on his shoulder, smiling at his grumpy tone. "Don't worry. You'll always be their favorite uncle."

He twisted his head to look down at me, his expression deadpan. "I better be, since Shawn's in Arizona and Liam's across the fucking globe."

"See?" I chirped. "You're already ahead of the game."

"I'll have you know, Doc's incredibly smart." He harrumphed as he watched Ainsley latch her arms around Koda's neck. "Sure, he's not tall . . . and he looks more like a box than a dog—"

"I always thought he resembled a rump roast with stubby little legs."

I had to curl my lips between my teeth to keep from laughing at my brother's glare. "My dog's just as good as that one." He threw his chin in Koda's direction with a sneer. "You'll see. You'll miss Doc in no time."

I nodded. "Of course," I said solemnly, all the while thinking I highly doubted that.

I SET the box I was holding down on the bed and looked around the room I'd be calling my own for the foreseeable future. Puffing out my cheeks, I blew a hard breath out past my lips as I tried to convince myself that this was the right decision.

"Am I making a huge mistake?" I asked Sunny when she crossed the threshold and put the box she was carrying down on top of the dresser.

She placed her hands on her hips and followed my gaze as I traced it along the pale sage green walls. "Well, even if you are, I'd say it's too late to back out now. The guys already have the heavy stuff set up, and that was the last box. I don't think any of them are gonna want to hear that you changed your mind."

I shot my best friend a killing look. "Thanks a lot. You're a huge help."

She laughed and came up beside me, throwing her arm around my shoulders. "This isn't a mistake, babe. It'll be an adjustment, sure, but it's not a mistake. If you're second guessing, think about your kids' faces when they saw their new rooms."

I knew she was right. I'd felt it in my bones when

Rhodes opened the door to Adeline's bedroom, and my girl moved inside, standing in the middle of the space with the kind of smile I hadn't seen from her in months. She needed this. Even more than my other children, my middle girl needed to be where she could close everyone else out and get lost in the quiet for a little while.

"Besides," Sunny spoke, pulling me from my thoughts, "I'm pretty sure if you tried to separate Koda and Ains now, there'd be a mutiny."

"I'm just scared," I admitted on a whisper, blinking against the burn forming in the backs of my eyes. "I know this was the right choice for my children, but I don't know if it was the right one for me."

Sunny dropped her arm, coming to stand in front of me so she could take my hands in hers. "Oh, honey."

"I mean, it's him, Sun. It's Rhodes. I don't know if—" I stopped, swallowing against the tightness in my throat. "I don't know if I can go there again."

"Hey." She waited for me to lift my gaze to hers. "No one is saying you have to, okay? This move isn't about that. You've been through more in the past six months than any person should have to go through in their entire life. This doesn't have to be anything more than a fresh start."

"But what if he—?"

Her fingers clenched around mine. "He'll respect

that. I know he will. Whatever you want—or don't want —he'll respect."

I could see something dancing in her gaze. The wheels in her head were spinning. "Why do I have a feeling there's a 'but' coming?"

She grinned, letting out a little giggle. "*But*," she said teasingly, "if you *did* decide you wanted to see where things went with my brother, you wouldn't hear any complaints from me."

"Sunny," I said in a warning tone, stepping away and dropping my head back with an exasperated groan.

"I'm not trying to pressure you." She held her hands up in surrender. "I'm not even going to mention how I always wished you could be my sister."

A sound a lot like a small grown rumbled from my chest. "You really aren't helping."

"I'm kidding!" she laughed, then, a second later, the humor died away. "Neither of you are the same people you were back then, B. I'm not going to make excuses for what he did when you were younger. I still want to kick his ass whenever I think about it. But he's changed. So have you. You were the softness he needed back then to round out his hard edges, but . . . maybe, this time around, he can be the softness you need."

I raised my brows. "Are you saying I've gotten hard?"

Her eyes filled with sympathy. "Honey, there's no

way a person can live through what you've lived through and not harden at least a little."

I sniffled, hating how right she was. I didn't feel like the same person I'd been before Elliott died. "But . . . what if I can't bring myself to trust him again?"

"There isn't a woman in the world who wouldn't understand that. But you don't have to give that out freely. It's his job to earn it."

For the millionth time in my life, I thanked whatever higher power had brought Sunny into my life and made her my best friend.

"When did you get so damn smart?"

"Puberty, I think. It was the strangest thing. It makes us girls smarter, but it turns boys into dumbasses."

I let out a laugh and pulled her into a hug, grateful beyond belief that she had the power to make me laugh, even in the hard times when I didn't think it was possible.

# Chapter Seventeen

## Rhodes

Less than a second after a knock sounded on my office door, it was pushed open and Marco came sauntering in. He sat in the chair across from me, casually leaned back, and kicked his cowboy boots up on the edge of my desk, all without saying a word.

My brows hitched up and a grin pulled my lips wide. "You forget this isn't your office anymore? Ah, shit. I don't have to tell Gypsy your mind's slippin' do I?"

He chuckled, shooting me the middle finger as he scooted lower in the seat to get even more comfortable. "Still such a shithead." He shook his head good-naturedly. "You know, I can still beat your ass if I have to."

I didn't doubt that for a single second. I might have

been Army just like he was, but I never made it to Rangers like him. My brother-in-law wasn't an example of a badass. Like Linc and all the rest of the men he worked with back when he'd been here, they were the very definition of the word.

"Guess that means you aren't goin' senile, then."

"Not just yet. Just wanted to swing by and see how things were goin'."

I knew a lot better than that. He was here to grill me for information, most likely at the request of Gypsy. It had been a week since Blythe and her kids had moved in with me, and my big sister had already called at least three times, asking when they'd be joining us for family dinner. "Uh-huh. And I guess you're gonna say next that my sister didn't put you up to this little visit?"

He lifted his shoulders in a shrug. "What can I say? I've never been good sayin' no to that woman."

That was no lie. Since coming into her life, there wasn't a damn thing Gypsy could want that he didn't bend over backward to find a way to give her, and I was hard-pressed to find a person who deserved it more. My sister had sacrificed everything to take care of us, to love us and support us and raise us. She did without in order to make sure we didn't, and one of the happiest days of my life was when she met Marco, because it meant she never had to do without again.

"Then you can be the one to tell her I'm not pushin' Blythe or her kids to come to dinner. I'm still trying to make sure they're comfortable. I'm not gonna risk spookin' them this early in the game."

He quirked a brow. "Spookin' *them* or spookin' *her?*"

I didn't bother answering. He already knew, he just wanted to give me shit about it. "I'm waiting until it stops feelin' like she's still got one foot out the door. Can you blame me?"

There wasn't a single thing in this world I wanted more than I wanted Blythe. She was it for me. If I couldn't have her, there would be no other woman. But this wasn't going to be easy.

"Look, Rhodes, I know what it's like to have to fight for the woman you love. Some days feel like the hardest battle of your life. Just don't give up, son. I understand why you let her go. Didn't agree with you, but I understood. It's hard to believe you're good enough for a woman like that when you were taught otherwise by parents who never deserved the title. By asshole kids who were raised by small-minded people to believe they were better than anyone who had less than them. But you've always been good enough for her, Rhodes. You were then, and you are now."

My ribs squeezed the hell out of my chest, making it hard to breathe. Marco was the man I respected most in the world, and hearing that from him meant more than if it had come from anyone else. "I know that now. Or at least I'm starting to. I'd like to think we would have lasted the long haul, but the truth is, I'm not sure we would have made it. I needed to do a lot of work on myself if I wanted a shot at making her happy forever." I scrubbed a hand down my face. "Just fuckin' hate that I hurt her the way I did."

"You'll have to show her you deserve another shot. But I have no doubt you can do that."

I was glad he believed in me. I wished I had the same confidence in myself. However, what I lacked there, I made up for with hope.

"I'm playing the long game here, Marco, and my sister isn't exactly known for her patience."

That got a smile out of him. "I'll do what I can to hold her off for as long as I possibly can, but you know your sister."

I heaved out a sigh. "Yeah, I know," I grumbled. "Do what you can."

The phone on my desk rang as he laughed, and I hit the button to answer it on speaker. "Bradbury."

Naomi's voice carried through the office. "Hey, Rhodes. You've got someone up front to see you."

My brows pinched together. "A meeting? I don't have anything on the calendar."

"Uh, no . . . She's a walk-in. Name's Grace."

*Ah shit.* That was the last thing I wanted on my bingo card for the day.

"Yeah, okay. I'll be right there."

Marco stood from his chair as I rose from mine and hit the button to end the call. "I'd say that's somethin' you need to deal with pretty quick, son. Situation like that could pop back up and bite you in the ass if you aren't careful."

An exhale burst past my lips. "Believe me, I know."

We said our goodbyes quickly, and I walked him out before heading toward the couches in the waiting room. "Hey," I greeted as I closed the distance and Grace rose from one of the two couches that faced each other.

"Hi," she said brightly, her eyes trailing to the big picture windows that overlooked the street, following Marco as he headed for his SUV. "That was your brother-in-law, right?"

She already knew he was. It was a small town, everyone knew most everything about everybody. But I knew why she was asking. He'd been right there, only feet away, and she'd been itching for an introduction. The fact that I wouldn't take her to meet my family when we were dating had been another argument we had more than once.

"It was. What can I do for you?"

She finally turned her attention to me, smiling brightly and batting her eyes. "I came to see if you wanted to grab some lunch. I don't know about you, but I could really go for a burger from Evergreen. Maybe follow that up with something sweet from Muffin Top?"

She'd just named the two places in this town that were guaranteed to be packed at this time of day, and she'd done it for a reason. She knew we'd be seen, and she knew word would spread. If I had to guess, she was here because she'd already heard people talking about my past with Blythe and the speculation on when or if we'd get back together, so she felt time was running out to shoot her shot.

I pushed out a sigh and rubbed at the tension building in the back of my neck and shoulders. "Grace, I don't think that's a good idea."

"Oh, well, if it's a timing thing, we could grab something to go. My schedule's flexible. I thought it would be nice to catch up."

The waiting room was empty, aside from Naomi sitting at the front desk, but this wasn't a conversation I wanted to have with any kind of audience. "Why don't you come back to my office real quick?"

Her smile told me she thought she was getting somewhere, which made my stomach sour. She was a good woman, I didn't want to keep hurting her, and I felt like an asshole because I knew that was what was about to happen.

I stepped aside so she could enter, then followed after her, making sure to close the door so no one could overhear. "Grace—"

"If you're busy, I totally understand. If you can't do lunch then maybe we could go out for dinner?"

"No, Grace, listen." I sucked in a fortifying breath. "I mean I don't think it would be a good idea . . . ever."

My stomach dropped as realization dawned in her eyes and the excitement turned to sadness. "I thought we were good. Weren't we good? I mean, we had fun together."

"We did. But it just isn't in the cards for us. I'm sorry."

"But . . ." She took a step closer and placed a hand on my chest, "It could have been if you'd given me half a chance. It still could be," she insisted, forcing a smile.

Christ, I was such an asshole. "Grace, you're an incredible woman, and you deserve a man who knows exactly how lucky he is to have you. That man isn't me. It can't be me."

She pulled her bottom lip between her teeth and bit down, her chin trembling. "It's because of Blythe, isn't it? Because she's back?"

I'd ended things with Grace before I knew Blythe

was returning to Hope Valley. When I realized my feelings for her weren't strong enough, and they weren't going to get any stronger. But I didn't say any of that because the first half of what she said was right. It was because of Blythe, and it always would be.

"Why are you willing to try again with her but not me?"

I gave her the truth. She deserved that much. "Because she owns my heart. She has since I was seventeen years old, and she always will. Whether or not she's ever mine again."

Grace sniffled, her eyes growing glassy with tears as she looked away. "I see," she whispered, a single tear breaking free and trailing down her cheek right before she turned on her heel and walked out of my office without another word.

Guilt ate at me, weighing heavily on my chest and shoulders for the rest of the day. That pressure stayed for hours, to the point I wasn't sure it would ever go away. Then the most miraculous thing happened.

The instant I pushed through my front door that evening, the weight lifted. It was a combination of things. The smell of something delicious cooking in the kitchen. The sight of Adeline sitting in the great room off the kitchen, curled up in a cushy wingback chair with a book in her lap. It was the sound of Ainsley singing off key and at an ear-splitting volume to whatever princess movie was playing on the television in the living room. And it was seeing Avett, his pockets stuffed full of treats, working with Koda, going through some of the training techniques I'd shown him. She already knew all of them, but it was fun for the both of them, so I didn't say anything. I didn't even say anything about the pink and purple bows and clips in the shape of butterflies the girls had clipped all over her long fur, though it severely impacted my dog's scary, badass vibe.

But mostly, it was rounding the corner and seeing Blythe in my kitchen, her feet bare and her work scrubs replaced with comfortable clothes. It was watching her hips swaying and her lips moving to whatever song was playing from her cellphone on the counter as she went about making dinner.

She belonged here. They all did. And seeing them in my house, filling it with noise and activity for the first time since I moved in, nothing in my life had ever felt more right.

# Chapter Eighteen

## Blythe

I hummed along to Shania singing about feeling like a woman as I moved around the kitchen, finally familiar enough with it to know where everything was—mostly because Rhodes gave me the freedom to move things to make them convenient for me.

Tristan's kitchen had been nice, but his house was older and closed-concept, making it more difficult to work in because it was cramped and impossible to keep an eye on my kids while I was cooking. I had to constantly stop to check and make sure one of them wasn't injured or bleeding.

Here, I could see every room from where I was standing at the massive stone island, chopping shallots and mincing garlic for the sauce I was preparing. I couldn't remember the last time I felt this relaxed. And it helped that my babies seemed to be settling into our new normal.

"Blythe, I told you, you don't have to cook."

I jolted at the sound of his voice and jerked around, the chef's knife in my hand swinging. "Jesus." I placed my free hand over my racing heart like that might slow it down. "You scared the shit out of me. I didn't hear you come in."

He moved forward, his steps hesitant, hands up in surrender as he eyed the knife with a quirked brow. "Clearly. But how about you put that knife down before you accidentally do some damage?"

I scrunched my lips to the side and gave him a baleful look. "Trust me, if I wanted to do damage, I would have. I know how to handle a knife." To prove my point, I turned back to the cutting board and went to work on the shallot, slicing and chopping it into precise, perfect little pieces before scooping them with the flat of the blade and dumping them into the simmering sauce.

When I turned back to Rhodes, he was grinning from ear to ear. All full lips, white teeth, and dark stubble. "I can see that," he said, appearing impressed with my knife skills. "And it smells incredible in here. But like I said, you don't have to cook."

My son came bouncing into the kitchen, buddying up to Rhodes. "Uncle Tris says Momma is a stress-cooker and it's your turn to have your freezer stuffed with a year's worth of leftovers."

I shot my son a scowl as I silently plotted how I was going to get back at my brother. It couldn't be something long-lasting or destructive. We weren't kids anymore, and as adults, that kind of thing was considered assault. I'd have to get creative.

The frown on Rhodes's face pulled me from my malicious musings. "Stress-cooking?" He took a step closer to me, concern radiating from his amber eyes. "Angel, are you stressed?"

"No," I assured him. Actually, this was the least stressed I'd been in months. "Okay, yes. I sometimes use cooking as an outlet," I confessed. "But that's not what this is. Honestly, I like doing it." I enjoyed coming up with creative recipes from the stuff in the fridge and pantry. I liked experimenting with flavors. And mostly, I liked feeding my family, seeing the way their eyes flared when they took their first bite of something they really enjoyed. I thrived on my children's appreciation and enthusiasm for my meals, and now I thrived on Rhodes's as well. "This is my happy place," I said, holding my arms out to indicate the kitchen. "I cook because it *helps* with stress, but also because I want to sometimes. Believe me, if I'm not in the mood, you'll be my first call to stop on your way home to grab pizza or takeout."

His eyes flared and his eyelids lowered to half-mast as he stared at me. I had a feeling it was because he liked me calling this place home. It had been a slip-up, but the truth was, the longer we were here, the more it *was* starting to feel like home. The kids had made the bedrooms their own, decorating how they wanted, and Rhodes had promised he'd take them to the hardware store to get paint and help them paint their rooms whatever colors they wanted. My children were happy. They were finally settled, and despite having Rhodes on my mind so much I was starting to dream about him at night, I was settled too.

The worry faded from his handsome features, and the smile that made my belly flutter returned. "All right. If it's what you want to do, I get it. Now, tell me how I can help."

"I want to help too!" Avett declared.

I gave them tasks, and together, the three of us made a delicious meal.

DINNER at the dining table had become the norm at Rhodes's house over the past week. Every night, we gathered around the long, rectangular table and ate together, filling each other in how our days had been and listening as the kids entertained us. It was nice. *Really* nice.

Back in Indiana, I tried to make sure we ate together as a family, but it never failed that Elliott would have papers to grade or a reason he had to head back to his office on campus—though, now I knew where he was really going whenever that happened. I'd always loved having dinner with my kids, but there had been an undercurrent of loneliness. That loneliness wasn't there any longer, and I had a feeling it was because of the man who sat across the table from me every night, no matter how tired or busy he was.

Dinner had gone off without a hitch. As usual, the kids had chattered away, filling Rhodes and me in on all the wild, crazy, exciting experiences they lived through at school and daycare. Given some of their stories, you would have thought they were the Goonies, living through crazy adventures on a daily basis.

After dinner, I got them upstairs and managed to get them bathed, their teeth brushed, and all of them in PJs with minimal fuss. It helped that, since turning nine, Avett had decided he was practically grown now and wanted to do everything on his own. It had broken my heart at first that my little boy was growing so fast and didn't need me as much as he used to, but I was trying hard not to hold on too tightly and let him spread his wings.

I had to read Ainsley's favorite bedtime story about a magical princess who rode her magical unicorn around, saving the kingdom from an evil witch—because of course my youngest didn't want to read about damsels-in-distress, she'd much rather read about the princess saving herself and everyone else—twice before she finally passed out.

I pushed her wild hair back and pressed a kiss to her forehead as I pulled the covers up around her and tucked her in tight. I flipped the switch so the only light in the room came from the fairy lamp on her bedside table and stepped out into the hall. I was about pull the door closed when the click of nails on the floor beside me caught my attention.

Koda's fluffy tail swished back and forth lazily as she stared up at me with her tongue lolling out the side of her mouth. I let out a little laugh. "I take it this means you're in here tonight?"

She opened her mouth and panted, and I could have sworn the dog looked like she was smiling. Over the past week Koda had bounced from one room to another, switching which of my kids she slept with each night. Looked like tonight was Ainsley's turn.

I pushed the door wide, and she skirted past me, her

feet soft like she knew she needed to be quiet. She really was the smartest dog. She climbed onto the little twin bed one paw at a time and inched her way up until my baby girl moved in her sleep, rolling over and throwing her tiny arm around Koda's neck in a hug. In return, Koda let out a pleased doggy huff and nuzzled down, passing out in a second.

I smiled, my chest feeling tight and warm as I took them in for a few heartbeats before heading farther down the hall toward Adeline's room. She was sitting up in her bed, her most recent book open in her lap, when I walked in. My little thinker had been reading above her class's level as long as she'd known how to read, and she'd gotten really big into chapter books lately.

"Hey, sweetie. You settled in?"

She smiled up at me softly. "Yeah, Mommy."

I moved closer, pulling her blankets up and tucking them around her tightly until she started giggling. "You're making me into a burrito, Mommy."

"Sure am, snuggle bug." Once I had her all wrapped up, I sat down on the edge of her bed and picked up the little clock on her nightstand, setting the timer for fifteen minutes. "You know the rules."

She nodded. "Fifteen more minutes of reading time, then bed."

"That's my girl." I leaned forward and kissed her forehead. "I love you, honey."

"Love you too, Mommy."

I stood up and started toward the door when she spoke again. "Mommy?"

"Yeah?"

"I'm really happy here." Her expression grew inquisitive. "Are you happy here?"

"I am," I answered honestly, my voice thick with emotion at the realization I'd done right by my children by moving them here. "Sleep good, snuggle bug."

When I got to Avett's room, he was sitting on the edge of his bed, staring unseeing at the wall across from him. I rapped my knuckle on the doorframe before stepping inside. He blinked his eyes clear and looked up at me, his features drawn together with sadness. "Hey, buddy. Everything okay?"

He lowered his head, his fingers tangling together in his lap. I pushed away from the door at the sound of his sniffle and rushed to him, sitting down on the bed beside him. A single tear fell and dripped down onto his pajama pants. "Oh, honey." I wrapped an arm around his shoulders and pulled him against me. "What's going on?"

"Do you—?" He let out a stuttered breath that felt

like a dagger right to my heart. "Do you think Dad's up in heaven mad at me?"

The air whooshed out of my lungs when he tilted his head up at me, his velvety brown eyes glistening with tears. The ache in the center of my chest was a very real, physical thing. "Baby, why would you think he'd be mad at you?"

"Because I realized at dinner that I'm not as sad as I used to be. I don't want him to think that I'm not sad 'cause I don't miss him. 'Cause I still miss him."

"Oh, baby. Of course, you still miss him."

"Then how come I'm not sad anymore?"

My throat tightened, but I still managed to get out, "Well, that's because you're healing. You'll miss your dad for the rest of your life, and some days you'll feel sadder than others, but as time passes, your heart heals and you're able to live your life and be happy and do all the things you did before."

He sniffled again, wiping his cheeks dry with the back of his hand. "Is it like that for you?"

I smiled, shoving down the anger I still felt at Elliott's betrayal. As hurt and mad as I was, I would never tarnish his memory. He might have turned out to be a terrible husband, but he'd always been a good father, and I wouldn't take that away from them.

"Yes, baby. That's what it's like for me too. And for

your sisters. And I'll tell you something else I know." I hugged him tighter. "Your Daddy's up in heaven right now, looking down on you kids, and he's so happy you and your sisters are healing. He never liked it when you guys were sad."

"He didn't," Avett agreed. "He always said it made him sad too."

"Exactly. He'd want you to be happy. The best way you can honor your dad's memory is to grow up to live a long, happy life full of love and laughter."

My son's chest expanded on a deep breath as the sadness in his eyes faded away. "Okay, Momma. I'll be happy because that's what Dad would want."

Lowering my head, I pressed my lips to Avett's temple and squeezed my eyes closed as I breathed him in. "I think that's a wise choice," I finally said when I pulled away. "Now get some sleep, yeah? It's been a long day."

He crawled to the center of his bed so I could tuck him in. After another kiss, I flipped off his bedside lamp and started for the door. "I think Dad would really like Rhodes," Avett said, drawing me up short.

I slowly turned, looking back at my boy from over my shoulder. "Oh yeah? Why's that?"

"Because he's funny and smart and cool and he makes us laugh," my insightful son said before showing just how wise he was by adding, "And you weren't happy for a really long time. Then we came here to live with Rhodes, and you were happy again. If Dad would want us all to be happy, he'd have to like Rhodes, 'cause Rhodes makes you happy."

I turned all the way around, taking in my son who was no longer a little boy. "I love you with all my heart. You know that? You and your sisters are the most important things in my life."

He hit me with a snaggle-toothed grin that melted my heart. "Yeah, Momma. I know. I love you too."

# Chapter Nineteen

Blythe

I headed downstairs, in desperate need of a glass of wine after my conversation with Avett. I knew my son was smart, but he was much more insightful than I gave him credit for.

When it came to being a mom, I'd really lucked out. Maybe I was partial, but I couldn't help feeling like I had the best kids on the planet.

My bare feet padded quietly against the floor as I moved to the kitchen for the bottle of wine I'd opened earlier with dinner. But instead of an empty kitchen like I expected, Rhodes stood at the sink, his back to me as he scrubbed the dirty dinner dishes.

He was dressed in a pair of light grey sweats that rested precariously low on his hips and nothing else. His hair was still damp from a shower, and beads of water dripped off the ends, trailing through the muscles that danced across his back as he moved around, scrubbing and rinsing and drying one dish at a time.

It was mesmerizing, and I couldn't help but stare, transfixed, at all that hard, toned, tan skin on display. I knew Rhodes was seriously built, but I had no idea a back could be *that* ripped. I wasn't sure I'd survive if he were to turn around and give me a look at the front, but my curiosity was more than piqued. It refused to be ignored.

"You know, you didn't have to do that," I said, finally alerting him to my presence. He grinned playfully over his shoulder, and I had to lock my knees to keep from melting into the floor when he shot me a wink. "I intended to do those tomorrow. And I planned to use your dishwasher, not wash them by hand."

His chuckle filled the otherwise quiet kitchen. "You know the rules, Blythe. You do the cookin', I do the cleanin'. It's only fair."

I barely heard a word that passed his lips after *you know*, because he'd chosen that moment to turn and face me in all his shirtless glory. First I'd been mesmerized by the way his biceps curled and his forearms bulged as he dried a water glass with a hand towel. Then my eyes snagged on the rows of ab muscles that lined his taut stomach. But as my gaze trailed up to his chest, everything in me froze, from the blood in my veins to the air in my lungs. Because right there, in the very center of his defined pec, above his heart, was a tattoo.

A pair of wings. Angel wings, to be exact.

My heart began to race as a burn built in my lungs, forcing me to let out the breath I'd been holding and suck in another one.

"Blythe?"

I blinked, dragging my attention to his face. "Sorry, what?"

One corner of his mouth was hooked up in a smirk. "You okay? You spaced out there for a few seconds." His expression and tone dripped with cockiness that had me rolling my eyes.

I pushed the meaning of the tattoo to the back of my mind. At least for now. I unstuck my feet from the floor and rounded the island to grab the wine bottle. "I'm fine, just came in for a glass of wine," I said as I poured.

Rhodes placed the sparkling clean glass in its cabinet and hung the dish towel over the handle of the oven door before turning to me, bracing his palms behind him on the counter and making the muscles in his chest pop.

"I was about to go sit out on the back porch if you feel like joinin' me. The view of the stars from there is unrivaled. Only place better is the lookout."

That had always been one of my favorite things

about Rhodes's and my secret spot. The view during the day was breathtaking, but at night, it felt like you were lying beneath a literal blanket of stars.

"Yeah, okay. That sounds good."

He brightened at that. Pushing off the counter and circling the island, he said, "All right then. I'll grab a shirt and meet you out there."

I moved to the hall closet for a light cardigan to pull on over my PJs. The nights were crisp in the mountains, and there wasn't much material to the satin shorts and camisole set I'd changed into before tucking the kids in.

With my wine in hand, I opened the sliding glass door to the back porch and stepped onto the chilled wood planks. The only place to sit was on the massive swing bolted into the roof of the porch, so I took a seat on the far end, curling my legs beneath me and pressing against the pillows propped against the arm and back. Sure enough, millions of stars blinked up in the dark sky, and I tipped my head back, taking them in as a breeze danced over me, blowing my hair across my shoulders and sending goosebumps across my skin.

The door slid open again a few minutes later, and Rhodes stepped out, feet still bare, gray sweats still on, only now he'd added a black cotton shirt that molded to him like a second skin. One side of my brain mourned the loss of all that naked flesh, but the other side of my brain was grateful, because that tattoo was currently living rent-free in my head, and I didn't think I had the bandwidth to get into the meaning of it just then.

Rhodes sat against the other arm, mindful to keep space between us, and kicked off with his foot, sending us back and forth in a slow, calming rock.

We sat in silence for a few minutes, enjoying the peace that came with being this far away from other people. The sounds of the forest were our playlist, the call of the night birds, the chirp of the crickets, the rustling of the trees as the wind slid through their branches.

"Kids get to bed okay?" he asked once I'd drunk half my glass.

That was a question he'd asked every night since we moved in, and I could tell by his expression that it wasn't a filler question. He really wanted to know. It mattered to him that my kids were comfortable and sleeping well. I could see that in his unwavering patience whenever Avett peppered him with a million eager questions, or how he didn't bat an eye when Ainsley demanded he have a tea party with her. It was in how he sat silently with Adeline while she read, reading a book of his own in complete silence while still providing her company. It was especially evident in the way he didn't seem to care that my girls were determined to make Koda into the fluffiest, biggest purse dog in existence, complete with bows and sparkly jewels.

I closed my eyes and rested my head against the back of the swing, letting the cool air caress my skin. "They did. Avett had a little crisis of conscience, but I think he's okay now."

The swinging stopped abruptly, forcing my eyes open and my gaze to his. From the faint light glowing through the window from inside, I could see that his features had grown serious. "Is he okay? Is there anything I can do?"

I let out a breath and took another sip of wine. "He's good now. He was worried what it meant that he wasn't as sad about his father passing as he had been when it was still fresh."

"Christ," he grunted. "Poor kid."

"I explained it was all a part of healing. That we aren't meant to stay sad forever. They've handled this loss with so much grace it's easy to forget how young they are sometimes."

"They've handled it so well because they have an incredible mom to guide them through."

My chest tightened and my eyes burned, but I managed to battle back the emotion, twisting my neck around to give him an appreciative smile. "Thank you for saying that," I said in a hushed voice. "I think I needed to hear it. Truth is, I've been questioning the job I've been doing lately."

He set us to swinging again. "You shouldn't. From everything I've seen, you're nailing it."

I let out a self-deprecating scoff as I looked out to the trees. "I wouldn't say I've been nailing it. More like muddling my way through. I got too wrapped up in my grief when Elliott died. Then all his secrets started coming to light just as I'd finally gotten my head above water. I let that consume me for too long, and I worried they had suffered for it."

His fingers caressed beneath my chin, turning my face and tilting it back so I met his eyes. Fire licked deliciously at my skin where he touched, and it took everything I had not to scoot closer to him on the bench.

"Hey, don't do that," he ordered in a tone that was somehow gentle and firm at the same time. "Don't downplay what you went through. Being a mother doesn't mean you don't get to grieve just because you have other people to be responsible for. You lost too, and you lost more. It wasn't just about him dying, you also had to deal with him not being who you thought he was. You're allowed to feel that too."

My breathing picked up and my heart began to race as his eyes held me captive. His words burrowed through my skin and into my chest, filling some of the places that had felt hollow for so long now.

"Thank you," I whispered, those two words laced with everything I was feeling.

Silence wrapped around us, creating a bubble only we were allowed in. The apple in his throat moved on a thick swallow, causing my mouth to go dry. My tongue peeked out to slide across my bottom lip, drawing his gaze to my mouth.

For a second I could have sworn he was going to kiss me, and I didn't know what the hell I was going to do if he did. But then his hand fell away and he scooted back across the bench.

The bubble had been popped, and it took a moment for me to catch my breath from what had happened.

I cleared my throat, taking another swallow of wine and returning to my study of the shadows the trees cast in the moonlight.

"So," I started once my heartrate finally returned to normal, then asked the first question to pop into my head. "How come you never settled down and had kids of your own?"

He brought a glass of what I knew was iced tea—since he didn't drink alcohol—to his lips, drinking back a healthy swallow of the amber liquid inside. I couldn't help but notice the way his fingers clutched the glass so tight his knuckles had turned bone white.

His jaw was tense and I could see the flutter of the pulse in his neck as I studied his profile. "Just wasn't in the cards for me, I guess."

I bit down on my bottom lip, unable to shake the sense there was more that he wasn't saying. "That's a shame. You're really great with my little band-of-chaos monsters."

He cast a quick grin in my direction before looking back out at the night. "Yeah, well, your kids are pretty damn incredible. It would be impossible not to like them."

My belly fluttered and my heart did a little flip.

"There was never anyone serious?" I didn't know why the hell I was pushing all of a sudden. I couldn't seem to help myself. "What about that woman from the grocery store? Looked like you guys might have had something at one time." A nasty, oily sensation coated my skin as I thought back to how she'd looked at him. I'd never considered myself a jealous person, but there was no other explanation for the way I was feeling.

"Grace?" His brows furrowed as he twisted in my direction and let out a little laugh. "No. We dated for a few months, but we were never that. It wasn't serious."

I thought back to the way her face lit up when she

saw him, then to how she reacted when I introduced myself. "Did she know it wasn't that serious?"

Rhodes heaved out a sigh and leaned forward, resting his elbows on his knees as he scrubbed at his jaw with his free hand. "I thought so. I was never anything but honest with her, but apparently, she had it in the back of her head that she could change my mind."

My mouth pulled into a wince. For Grace *and* for Rhodes. That couldn't have been a pleasant situation for either of them. "I'm sorry."

"Yeah," he sighed, "me too. She is a good woman. I just couldn't make it work."

I tried to tamp down my next question, but the words spilled out before I could swallow them down. "Why was that?"

His gaze collided with mine, no traces of humor in his eyes. "You know why, Blythe," he rumbled, his voice like gravel wrapped in silk.

My eyes widened and my lips parted on a gasp. The goosebumps that spread across my body had nothing to do with the temperature. "No, I—"

"Don't play that game. It's one thing if you don't feel it yourself, but don't pretend you don't know the truth. You saw the tattoo, for Christ's sake."

I couldn't catch my breath all of a sudden. The sound of his voice was all I could hear over the rush of blood in my ears. "Rhodes," I whispered, my fingers tensing with the need to reach out and touch him. But I held myself back.

"I never wanted to make it work with anyone else because they weren't you, Angel. It was you or no one. You married Elliott and had those incredible kids upstairs, so I chose no one."

I didn't know how the hell it was possible, but hearing him say that somehow broke my heart and stitched pieces of it back together at the same time. I shouldn't have liked hearing he was alone because he never stopped wanting me, but I did.

He lifted his glass and knocked back the rest of his tea like he wished it was something much stronger before standing from the swing. "I never regretted that decision, Blythe. Not for a single fuckin' minute, because I never stopped hoping that one day, you'd come back to me."

With that, he leaned down and hooked his hand behind my neck. My head tipped back and he pressed his full lips into the very corner of my mouth. "Sleep good, Angel," he said quietly, then he walked back into the house, leaving me reeling.

# Chapter Twenty

Blythe

The best of The Rolling Stones played through the speakers of my phone as I moved throughout the living room with furniture polish and a rag. It was one of the very rare days I was off work at the same time the kids were at school, so I had the whole house to myself. Well, Koda and me, but she was perfect company. Unless she needed to go outside, she stayed curled up in her dog bed and snoozed while I went about cleaning.

I lifted my hand and swiped at the beads of sweat on my forehead with the back of my wrist. When I first started, I hadn't given much thought to the size of his house, but the ache in my back and knees, and the sweat making my shirt stick to my body brought that to the forefront of my mind.

Well, second to the forefront, actually. The number one spot was designated for what had happened the night before with Rhodes on the back porch. I hadn't been able to stop thinking about what he said, that near kiss, or how all of it made me feel.

That was why I'd woken up and decided cleaning the house from top to bottom was a great idea—spoiler alert, it wasn't. I woke up feeling like my skin was two sizes too small. I was tense and twitchy. An anxious buzz thrummed in my veins, like I had bees beneath my skin. I'd needed to find something to do to occupy my time so I didn't spend the entire day thinking of how badly I wished Rhodes had kissed me, and calling Sunny wasn't an option. If I confessed what happened to my best friend, she'd get excited, and I didn't want to get her hopes up. Hell, I didn't want to get *my* hopes up.

I didn't have the first clue what I was doing, but I knew I was in trouble when I checked the clock for the third time in as many hours. I told myself I wasn't eagerly waiting for Rhodes to get home, but I was full of shit.

After cleaning the entire house, I somehow still had energy to spare, so I went through the kitchen and made an extensive grocery list. The local market had started making deliveries, so I called in everything I needed for meals for the next week, a few staples I had to keep on hand for the kids, and the stuff I'd seen Rhodes snacking on.

While I waited for my grocery delivery, I cleaned out the fridge, tossing out anything expired, and scrubbed down the shelves. I was just finished loading the last item back in its designated spot when the chime of the doorbell echoed through the house and sent Koda racing toward the door.

"Yeah, I heard it," I told Koda as she looked back and forth between me and the door, like she was trying to tell me there was someone on the other side. "You're the smartest girl in the whole wide world, aren't you?" I cooed as I twisted the knob and opened the front door.

Laughter died in my throat and my smile fell as soon as I looked up and saw who was standing on the front porch.

"Hi," I said, caught off guard at the sight of Grace standing in front of me. It took a moment to realize what she was doing here, then I noticed the reusable grocery bags hanging from her arms.

"Hi, um . . ." She tilted sideways and looked over my shoulder into the house. "Is Rhodes here? I have his groceries." She lifted her arms in indication.

"Oh, uh, no. He's at work. Those are actually mine."

The tension in the air grew even thicker when her

brow furrowed in confusion. "If they're yours, why are they . . .?"

She trailed off, not saying another word until I was forced to break the silence. "Yeah, my kids and I moved in a little over a week ago."

The color drained from her face as her lips parted in shock. "You're living here," she repeated quietly.

"Um . . . yeah." This whole situation was getting more awkward by the second. "Here, let me help—"

She jerked the bags away when I reached out to take them from her. "It's fine," she said, her tone as hard as her expression. Her cheeks went from pale to flushed in just a few seconds. "It's my job."

"Sure . . . okay." I stepped aside, unsure what else to do. I didn't necessarily want her inside, given the sudden shift in her demeanor, but I also needed those groceries, and there was no way in hell I'd be going back to Fresh Foods and risk another run-in with her.

She moved through the house like she was familiar with it, going straight to the kitchen and placing the bags on the island.

"There are a few more in the car," she muttered on her way past. "Be right back."

I looked down at Koda with wide eyes. "What the hell was that about?" I whispered to her. She quirked her head in response like she was just as confused as I was.

Since she wasn't going to let me help her carry bags in, I started to unload the ones on the island, placing items where they belonged.

"You've really made yourself at home, haven't you?"

I set the can of refried beans I'd just grabbed back on the counter and turned to look at her as she dumped the last of my groceries on the island. "Excuse me?"

She waved a hand around the kitchen, then into the living room. Rhodes had told me and the kids to make this place our home, so that was what we'd done. Aside from the pictures he had on the mantel, there wasn't much in the way of decoration, so I'd hung some of the paintings I had in storage. The oversized chenille blanket stretched across the back of the couch was mine, as were the decorative throw pillows and the rug beneath the coffee table.

Avett's tennis shoes were by the door, and there was a basket of Ainsley's favorite toys in the corner by the window. The house felt lived in and homey, something that had been missing before, and clearly, the woman standing in front of me wasn't happy about it.

"I'm sorry. Have I done something to offend you?"

Her lips pulled into a sneer. "No, of course you haven't." When she spun around and started out of the house, I followed with the intension of shutting and locking the door behind her. Only, before she made it onto the porch, she stopped and turned around. "You know, I could have made him happy."

I rocked back on my heel with the force of her words and the anguish in her eyes. "What?"

"Rhodes. I could have really made him happy. If he had given me the chance, I know I could have."

My heart ached for her. Whatever feelings Rhodes had for her, Grace's had been so much more for him. He might have played it down, saying it had only been a few months, but it was obvious in that short time, she'd fallen in love with him. I knew all too well what it felt like to be hurt by the person you loved. I'd lived it more times than I cared to mention.

"Grace, I'm really sorry—"

"You should be." She let out a watery laugh that held a hefty amount of pain and blinked up at the ceiling, fighting back tears. "I tried everything to get him to let me in, but his heart was locked up so tight, I never had a shot. Because he's still wrapped up in you."

"My history with Rhodes is complicated," I defended, my pity quickly starting to morph into annoyance. "That's between him and me. And, no offense, but it's also none of your business."

She held her chin up, despite the way it trembled. "You're only going to end up hurting him. If you guys didn't work out the first time, what makes you think it'll work now, huh?"

I made sure to keep my voice calm as I replied, "I could ask you the same question, but I really don't care what you'd have to say about it. I don't want to be mean, because it's obvious you're hurting, and I can sympathize with that. Probably more than you can imagine. But you walked in here swinging, so it is what it is. You obviously have no idea about my history with Rhodes, and I'm not going to waste my time schooling you. Think what you want, but do it somewhere else, because this is my home, and it's time for you to go."

She sniffled at the same time her eyes narrowed into vicious slits. "I might not know your history, but I do know one thing. That man has been living half a life all these years, and he deserves better than that. If you aren't going to make him whole, you need to let him go so someone else has a chance to be that for him."

With that, she turned on her heel and stormed out, slamming the door behind her.

THE BELL over the door chimed as I pushed inside the salon. My mom paused in sweeping the loose hair at her station and turned my way, smiling brightly when she spotted me. "Blythe? Well, this is a pleasant surprise."

"Hey. I was hoping to catch you before you headed home." Because I needed her advice, and as much as I loved Trick like he was my own father, this wasn't a situation he could really help with.

Mom propped the handle of the broom against the ledge at her station and crossed her arms. "Is everything okay?"

I let out a sigh that sounded as heavy as it felt. I hadn't been able to stop thinking about what Grace said on her way out about Rhodes only living half a life, and with every passing minute, the weight on my chest grew. "I don't know, Mom."

She gave me that quintessential mother expression. It was one I hadn't fully understood until I became a mother myself, an expression that said she felt every single thing her child was feeling. "Come on back to the wash station, honey pie." She waved me forward. "I'll give you a nice head massage and blowout and you can tell me all about it."

My eyes welled up as I smiled. This was what she used to do whenever things got too hard for me to handle. She'd bring me here and wash my hair, lulling me into relaxation and making it easier for me to open up about what was wrong in my world.

The familiar sensation of her fingers combing through my hair and massaging my head took me back to my childhood. This was one of my happiest places outside of the lookout, and I was with the one person who always made me feel safest.

My eyes closed on a deep, soothing exhale as my mother worked my hair into a lather. "Talk to me, sweetheart. What brought you to my chair?"

"How did you know you were ready to let someone else in? I mean, after everything you went through with my father." I refused to call the man Dad. He'd lost the right to that title years ago.

She inhaled deeply, her gaze trailing off as she thought of how to answer. "It wasn't about knowing when I was ready. It was about meeting the man I couldn't stop thinking about, the man I wanted *despite* everything I had been through. When our divorce was finalized, I honestly didn't know if I would ever date again, but Trick made me so happy, I couldn't help but fall for him."

That hit me in the center of my chest. I thought about what Avett said the night before about being happy.

"It's just . . . after everything that happened, I don't know if I can trust myself again. My vision blurred with tears, one breaking free and trailing into the wet hair at my temple. My mother brushed it away with her knuckle before turning the water on to just the right temperature to rinse the shampoo from my hair.

"Oh, baby girl, I understand. Being cheated on can be a real blow to your self-esteem. And I can't imagine having to find out the way you did. I wouldn't fault you for wanting to keep your heart under lock and key. However, only you can decide if protecting it from ever being hurt again is worth being alone."

I spun those words around in my head as she conditioned my hair and rinsed again. Finally, she wrapped the wet ends in a towel and helped me sit up, coming around to crouch in front of me and take my chin between her thumb and index finger. "But I'll tell you something, I'd go through all that pain again and again if it led me to Trick. You and Tristan are the best things I ever created, but he's the best chance I've ever taken."

Another tear slipped free as I smiled at my mom. "I love that you found that."

"Me too, honey pie," she whispered. "And something tells me that, if you're willing to take the same chance, there's something just as special waiting for you. Most people are lucky enough to find love once. But then there are those of us who are blessed enough to get it twice in a lifetime. It would be a shame if you threw that way, don't you think?"

# Chapter Twenty-One



## Rhodes

The lights from inside burned brightly through the windows when I got home after an exhausting day, but when I pushed through the front door, I was met with silence.

I could smell the mouthwatering spices of whatever Blythe was making for dinner, but that was the only sign of life. Koda came scrabbling into the entryway to greet me, suspiciously alone when usually one of the kids came running over with her.

"Hello?"

Blythe's sweet voice called out, "In the kitchen."

I rounded the corner in time to catch a peek of her sweet, heart-shaped ass as she removed something from the oven and closed the door. "No way," I let out when she turned around and set the hot cast iron skillet on a trivet to keep it from damaging the stone. "You made steak?"

She looked almost nervous, chewing on her bottom lip as she studied the spread on the counter. "Yeah. Filets pan-seared and basted in herb butter, then finished off in the oven." She pointed to the other two dishes on the counter. "Along with roasted potatoes cooked in duck fat and infused with rosemary and garlic, and honey-glazed carrots."

I looked from the food to the woman, my jaw hanging open as I took her in fully for the first time since walking through the door. She was wearing a sweet little yellow sundress with a flow-y skirt that fell to mid-thigh. Her hair looked softer and shinier than usual and the skin on her shoulders, arms, and legs glowed. Her face was makeup-free, with the exception of a bit of mascara on her lashes. Not that she needed any of it. If anything, the makeup hid all the things I loved about her. I preferred to see the freckles that dotted her nose and the pretty pink flush on her cheeks.

She fidgeted in place, shifting anxiously on the balls of her feet, drawing my notice to the fact that she'd repainted her toes a sassy bright red at some point.

"Those are still all your favorites, right?"

They were, and she knew that. "They are. Where are the kids, Angel?"

She twisted her fingers together in a move I'd seen Avett do any time he got anxious or excited. "I asked my mom if they wouldn't mind keeping them, so they're having a sleepover with Nana and Pop-Pop."

Heat flooded my insides as the blood started pumping through my veins faster. I slowly started around the counter to her side. "And why did you do that?"

She pulled her lips between her teeth and bit down on them as her skin turned a brighter pink. She started moving back as I closed in on her, step by step, until her back hit the edge of the counter.

"I thought it would be a good idea for us to talk."

My heart threatened to beat out of my chest as I braced my hand on the counter on either side of her, trapping her in place. The tether I had on the hope I'd been feeling since Blythe moved back snapped. There was no controlling it anymore, no holding it back.

I leaned in and inhaled deeply, savoring the smell of amber and roses on her skin. "What do you want to talk about?"

"I want—well, maybe we should talk about us?"

Christ, was this really happening? I was almost too scared to believe it. But then those bright turquoise eyes of hers flashed to my mouth before her tongue slipped out to wet her lips, and my dick pulsed in my jeans. It was taking every bit of strength I had not to grab her and kiss her until neither of us could breathe.

"I didn't realize there was an 'us' to talk about."

When her teeth sank down on her plump bottom lip, I nearly lost hold of my sanity. "Do you want there to be?"

I shook my head, my face close enough the tip of my nose almost brushed against hers. "Nu-uh, Angel. None of that. I've been nothin' but honest with you. You know exactly how I feel and what I want. You need to tell me what you want."

I held my breath as I waited for her to say something. "I want there to be an us," she finally said, those Caribbean eyes glistening with emotion. "I want you, Rhodes."

I couldn't hold back for another goddamn second. I moved before she finished saying my name, slamming my lips on hers and banding an arm around her waist. My free hand tangled in her hair, wrapping the long strands around my fist so I could tip her head back and devour her sweet mouth. She rose on her toes to get closer, her arms wrapping around my shoulders as she opened her lips so I could push my tongue inside. A growl rattled through my chest when her nails dug into the back of my neck like she was afraid I'd disappear if she let go.

The kiss was hungry and primal and full of everything I'd felt for her for the past twenty years. I couldn't remember the last time I felt this desperate for something, and despite the fact I was holding her against me so tight not even light could get through, it still didn't feel close enough.

"God, I've missed you," I grunted against her silky skin as I dragged my lips down the column of her neck.

"Rhodes," she breathed, her voice low and throaty. I never thought I'd hear her say my name like that again, filled with desire and dripping with need. It made my cock twitch behind my fly like it was trying to stab its way through the denim to get to her.

"You have no fuckin' clue how bad I need you. How I've always needed you."

She fisted my hair and yanked my head back, those glassy turquoise eyes dark with lust. "I need you too. Now. Please, Rhodes."

There was nothing I'd deny this woman. I would happily spend the rest of my life giving her everything she could ever want. I wanted to reach beneath her skirt and rip her panties off so I could stuff her full of my cock, but I needed to make sure her head was in the same place mine was.

Pulling back, I broke the kiss, my chest swelling when she followed, chasing after my lips with a tiny growl like she couldn't get enough. She was as desperate for me as I was for her, and fuck if that didn't make me even harder.

I kept hold of the back of her neck with one hand while I placed the other on her right knee. I slowly dragged it upward as I locked her gaze with mine. "You need to be sure, Blythe."

She licked her kiss-swollen lips, her chest rising and falling with each frantic breath. "I'm sure."

"No, baby. If I take you now, that changes everything. You're mine. For good."

She let out a needy whimper as my hand slipped beneath the material of her skirt and continued on its journey up.

"I lost you twenty years ago, and I'm never letting that happen again. If you let me have you now, there is no going back."

"Rhodes, please touch me," she begged as I got so close that I could feel the heat of her pussy against my fingers.

"You and those kids are permanent," I explained at the same time I continued my tortuous caress. "*We* are permanent. Tell me you get that."

*Christ, please* I silently begged. *Please want that as well.*

Her hands came up and cupped my cheeks, pulling

my face close to hers. "I know what it means when I say I want you. I know this could never be casual or temporary. Not with you. You've always been special to me, Rhodes. Always. I've tried so hard not to love you—"

Her eyes widened as soon as she realized what she said. "Don't," I ground out, clenching my jaw and pressing the tips of my fingers into the flesh at the inside of her thigh. "Don't you try to take back what you just said." I squeezed my eyes closed and rested my forehead against hers. "Fuck, please don't take it back."

Her sweet breath gusted over my lips as she slid her fingers into the hair at my temples. "I'm not taking it back," she whispered so softly it was a wonder I could hear her over my heart pounding in my ears. "I tried not to love you, Rhodes. But I can't make myself stop."

"Say it," I commanded in a gruff, raspy tone as I slid my hand the rest of the way up her thigh and cupped her core, the heat of her beating against my palm. "Say it, and I'll give you what you want."

She braced her hands on my shoulders. "I love you." Her sentence ended on a gasp as I slipped the lace of her panties aside and shoved two fingers inside her. "Oh God," she cried out, her head falling back as I began a steady rhythm, pumping my fingers in and out of her tight, wet channel. Only seconds passed, but her walls were already fluttering around me.

I used my grip on the back of her neck to tilt her face back to mine. "Open your eyes, baby. Let me see you."

She peeled her lids up, only making it to half-mast. "Again," I ordered as I continued to feed my fingers in and out of her, picking up the pace and curling them to brush against that most sensitive place inside her.

"I love you, Rhodes," she repeated, her hips beginning to circle in time with each thrust of my fingers. "God, I love you. Please don't stop."

I brought my thumb into play, pressing it against her clit as she rode my hand harder, quickly losing control.

"I love you too, Angel," I grunted against her lips. "Never stopped."

Her eyes rounded as she panted, sharing the breath between us. "Kiss me," she pleaded, yanking me back to her before I had a chance to comply. As soon as my tongue swiped against hers, she exploded, clamping down around my fingers and crying out into my mouth as she rode out her orgasm, moaning over and over as I continued pressing against her G-spot and circling her clit, dragging her release out until her body collapsed against mine.

Pulling my fingers from inside her, I watched her as I parted my lips and licked off every drop of her arousal. The moment her taste exploded on my tongue, I knew I needed more.

"Baby, the dinner you made smells so good."

She gave me a lust-drunk smile. "Thank you."

"But we're gonna have to wait till breakfast to enjoy it, because if I don't fuck you in the next thirty seconds, my head'll explode."

"Wha—" Her question cut off on a yelp when I bent forward and tossed her over my shoulder. "Rhodes," she cried out, letting loose a sweet, musical laugh that filled my chest with warmth.

"First time I'm inside you again isn't gonna be on the kitchen counter. I want room to move around so I can fuck you all night long."

"Well, if you insist," she teased as I bounded up the steps. "Who am I to argue?"

She let out another peel of laughter when I turned my head and sank my teeth into the side of her ass cheek.

I would never get tired of hearing that sound, and I would do everything in my power to hear it again and again, every day for the rest of my life.

# Chapter Twenty-Two

## Blythe

The mood shifted the moment we entered Rhodes's bedroom. The atmosphere grew thick, the air crackled with electricity. The playful version from only a second ago disappeared, replaced with the serious Rhodes I knew all too well.

He lowered me to the floor, dragging me down his body at a torturously slow pace, teasing my painfully hard nipples by making sure they felt every single ridge and dip of muscle in his chest and stomach before brushing up against the steel rod of his erection.

His eyes had grown so dark they were nearly black as he stared down at me while holding me so tightly against him I could feel the thunderous beat of his heart as it banged against his ribs and rattled through my entire body.

His rough hands skated up my arms, his long, thick fingers toying with the thin spaghetti straps of my sundress before sliding them down my shoulders, pushing them down farther until the dress slipped free and the loose material pooled at my feet, leaving me standing in nothing but my lace thong.

Rhodes licked his lips as he stared at my tightly puckered nipples before dragging his gaze back up to my own. "No bra?" He quirked a brow.

The breath I released came out stuttered and choppy. "It didn't really work with the dress." There weren't many times I appreciated my smaller chest. Most of my life I'd wished the B cup I'd been given was a C. However, the fact that I could go braless more often than women who were more endowed was a silver-lining.

He let out a gruff hum of approval as his gaze returned to my breasts. "Fuck me, I never forgot how beautiful your tits were." As if to show how much he appreciated them, he cupped the one on the right and lowered his head, sucking the stiff peak between his lips and pulling so hard he wrenched a gasp from deep in my chest.

My head fell back at the delicious sting, my hands flying up so my fingers could tangle in his hair and hold him tightly while his sinful mouth continued to work. A sharp hiss slithered through my teeth when he bit down on the tip, but before it could really hurt, he laved at the sting with his tongue, soothing it before moving to the next and giving it the same treatment.

My core throbbed and pulsed, my walls fluttering around nothing, desperate to be filled as my hips began to rock forward, rubbing up against the erection pressed into my lower belly.

"Rhodes." My voice came out high-pitched and needy. "Please."

He released my nipple with a pop. "Please what, Angel?"

"I need more," I panted, my desperation so acute it bordered on insanity. I yanked at the material of his shirt like it had personally offended me, hating the layers of clothes he still wore while I stood in front of him, practically naked. "I want to see you."

An arrogant smirk pulled at his full lips as he reached behind his head and grabbed the collar of his shirt, yanking it off in a single motion. My pulse thrummed like the flutter of hummingbird wings at the sight of that tattoo, but my attention was quickly diverted when his fingers worked the button of his jeans free and slid the zipper down. He made quick work of kicking off his boots and toeing his socks off before shoving his jeans down and stepping out of them. The prominent bulge behind the tight black fabric of his boxer briefs made my mouth water. I wanted to drop to my knees and slide his cock into my mouth to see if he still tasted like I remembered.

But that would have to wait for another time. Right then I needed him inside me more than I needed my next breath.

I looked back up at him and quirked a brow. "All of you," I said, the command dripping from those words.

"Tit for tat, Angel. You wanna see all of me, you have to return the favor."

I didn't hesitate. I simply took a step back, slipped my fingers into the fabric at my hips, and pushed my thong down until I was completely bare to him.

"Fuckin' hell," he grunted, the amber of his eyes nearly swallowed up by his black pupils. "Still the prettiest pussy in the world.

I raised my chin, my chest swelling proudly. "Your turn," I challenged.

In less than a second, he shoved his underwear down and kicked them free, leaving him buck naked in the blink of an eye. His cock stood proudly between us, long and hard and thick, a pearly bead of pre-cum glistening from the very tip. I couldn't help but lick my lips at the sight of it.

"Baby, you keep looking at my dick like that and this is gonna be over before we really get a chance to start."

I forced my eyes back up to his and said the first thing that popped into my head. "I need all of you."

He reached down and took my wrist, guiding my hand up to settle on his pec, right over the pair of angel wings he had permanently etched into his skin. He pressed my palm against his heated skin right above his heart. "You have all of me, Blythe. Forever."

"And you have me," I whispered through the tightness in my throat. "Now I need you to fuck me like you've spent the last twenty years missing me."

At my command, he hooked his hands under the backs of my knees and hefted me up, forcing my legs to circle his waist as he put one knee, then the other, into the mattress and moved us to the center of the bed.

He laid me down, my head resting on the mound of pillows, and hovered over me. "Tell me you're safe, Angel, so I can take you bare. You have my word that I'm clean."

After Ainsley, I was done having kids, so I had my doctor put in an IUD. "I'm safe," I told him. And I had a checkup a couple months ago. I'm clean." I lifted a palm and caressed his cheek. "You can take me bare, Rhodes. I don't want anything between us."

He rested his forehead against mine for a moment as

he closed his eyes and breathed deeply before shifting his hips so the tip of his cock bumped against my entrance. "Watch me," he ordered as he slid the first inch inside me. "Watch me take you, Angel."

The breath stuck in my chest as I trailed my eyes down between our bodies and watched as he slid into me until he was fully seated, taking me completely for the first time in twenty years.

"Oh my God," I cried out, fighting against my body's reaction to drop my head back as he filled and stretched me. It wasn't just his cock filling me. It was him. Filling those places inside me that had felt hollow and cold for so long.

"Jesus," Rhodes grunted, pulling out, his length glistening with my arousal before sinking back inside me. "You feel so fucking perfect. Like your body was made to fit perfectly with mine."

"I'm so full." My words were followed by a whimper as he pulled out and glided back in. I lost sight of his cock when he slammed his lips down on mine, forcing my lips apart so he could thrust his tongue into my mouth in time with his hips as he picked up the pace, driving into me harder and faster. "Yes," I hissed as his long cock stroked against that spot deep inside that made every muscle in my body clench.

"That's it, baby," he coaxed, his gaze locked with

mine as he lowered down onto his forearms, giving me more of his weight. "Jesus, you feel so perfect. How hot and wet your pussy is. How tight you're squeezing me. You're taking me so good, baby. Such a good girl."

He hit that spot again and again as he moved his mouth down my neck, trailing kisses in his wake. The tension in my body snapped when I felt the drag of his teeth against my collarbone followed by a sharp sting when he bit down. That brief stab of pain, coupled with the delicious pressure building in my core, set me off.

My mouth dropped open on a wordless scream as every nerve ending in my body sparked to life. I felt everything so acutely, the drag of his chest against my nipples, the whisper of his breath on my skin, the pulse of his cock against the throbbing walls of my pussy. Everything pulled in, gathering in my center and building higher and higher until it could no longer be contained and burst outward, exploding like an unstable star.

Rhodes kissed me through every roll and peak of my release, swallowing my moans and unintelligible words until his cock swelled even thicker and his movements became uncoordinated and jerky. He tore his mouth from mine. "Fuck, *fuck*! I'm gonna come, baby." With that, he buried his face in my neck on a primitive groan as he came deep inside me.

He collapsed on top of me, banding his arms around me before rolling to his back with me draped on top of him. I nuzzled into his chest, letting out a sigh of deep, boneless contentment as I settled against him.

"I love you so fuckin' much," he breathed a few minutes later.

I turned my head, burying my smile against his skin. "I love you too," I whispered against his skin, joy building so large in my chest it felt like it would burst from the tips of my toes and fingers any second.

What Grace said earlier reverberated in my brain, and I lifted my head, propping my chin on the backs of my hands so I could look up at him. "Are you happy?"

He lifted an arm and folded it behind his head, propping himself up so he could see me. His brows pinched together as he reached down with his other hand and brushed the hair back from my face. "What?"

"Are you happy?" I repeated.

His features smoothed out, his expression growing tender as he traced my hairline with the tip of his finger. "Yeah, Angel. I'm very happy. Are you?"

"I am. Because you make me happy, Rhodes," I confessed. "And I want to make sure I give you the same. I—I don't want you living half a life."

Understanding filled his eyes. "I know it might have seemed to some people like all I've been doing all these years is existing, but I've had a good life with a family who loves me and I'm surrounded by good friends. I found my purpose in the Army, then again when I came back here. And I think we can both agree that I have the smartest dog in the world." He grinned as I let out a giggle. "No, I didn't get married or have kids because you were the only woman I ever wanted that with, but that didn't mean my life wasn't complete. I had everything I needed. You coming back into the picture gave me *more*. And this time around, I have the added bonus of those kids. I've lived a good life, baby. You'll never hear me complain. You make it even better."

Hearing that soothed the jagged pieces inside me. It settled the turmoil I'd been feeling since my run-in with Grace. Twisting my head, I pressed my cheek back into his chest and let out a happy sigh. "That was a really good answer," I said quietly, my body slowly succumbing to exhaustion from the workout it just had.

Rhodes's cheek shook on a silent laugh as he hooked an arm around me and hugged me tight. "I'm glad you approve. Now get some sleep, Angel. You need to rest up, because I'm nowhere near done with you."

# Chapter Twenty-Three

## Blythe

I could hear my co-workers whispering behind me, but I was too busy daydreaming to really pay attention to what they were gossiping about. I barely comprehended the words on the screen in front of me as I brushed my fingers over the mouse to scroll from page to page.

A throat cleared behind me, the sound so obnoxiously loud that it burst my happy little bubble and drew me back to the present.

I blinked and swiveled in my chair, facing Heather, Diana, and Gretchen. "What?" My gaze bounced between all three of them as they snickered. "What did I miss?"

"You've been in your own little world over there," Gretchen pointed out with a cheeky grin.

"Yeah," Heather added. "We've been trying to get your attention for five minutes now, but your head is so high in the clouds you couldn't hear us."

Diana waggled her brows, "Looks like someone got slammed nice and hard."

I choked on the sip of coffee I'd taken as Gretchen burst into laughter and Heather cut her eyes in her direction. "You don't have any kind of filter, do you?"

She lifted her chin proudly. "Nope? I am who I am."

"She has a point, though." Gretchen narrowed her eyes, studying me closely. "You're all glow-y and blissed-out this morning. Unless you found a new skincare serum that creates magic overnight, I can only think of one thing that makes a person look like that."

"Yeah, a nice, hard dicking."

"Diana!" I croaked out, nearly choking on *another* drink of coffee.

"Don't get all bashful now," Heather said in a scolding tone. "Not when you've got tea to spill."

"It's that guy who came in the other week, isn't it" Gretchen asked. "That really hot one with the killer smile?"

My face felt like it was on fire, and the blush gave me away before I could get a word out.

"It is!" Diana jabbed her finger in my face. "Look at her. She's blushing!"

"I'm not surprised. Aren't you living with the guy?" Heather asked.

"We were more like housemates," I explained. "But . . . things changed last night."

All three of them let out squeals of excitement that stabbed through the air like needles jabbing at my eardrums.

"How did it happen?" Gretchen asked.

"Yeah, tell us," Diana insisted. "Did the sexual tension get to be too much and you guys ripped into each other like rabid gorillas?"

My chin jerked back in shock. "As colorful as that visual is, no, it wasn't quite like that." Well, we ripped into each other, but it wasn't like rabid gorillas, that was for damn sure. "He and I actually dated for three years when we were younger." A dreamy smile tugged the corners of my mouth upward. "We were each other's first loves. And, well . . . other firsts."

Heather clasped her hand in front of her chest. "Oh my God, I love that. It's like a romantic movie come to life or something."

As if we'd spoken him into existence, the door opened and the man of the hour came walking in. The sight of him in those faded jeans and a cotton tee was enough to rev my engine in a very big way.

"Hey," I said, smiling brightly.

"Hey back, Angel."

"Gah, I love that he calls her Angel," I heard Gretchen mutter, but I couldn't pull my attention from the man in front of me.

He braced a forearm on the counter between us and lifted his hand, making a come-here motion with his finger. A girlish giggle worked its way up my throat as I pushed up from my seat and leaned across the counter so I could give him the kiss he so clearly wanted.

"This is a really nice surprise," I said. "What brings you by?"

He placed a familiar paper bag on the counter. The contents smelled so good they made my stomach growl. It wasn't until that moment I realized we didn't have dinner the night before or breakfast earlier that morning. We'd been too busy doing other things to think about food. "Thought you might want some lunch. Evergreen's California Club and Tomato Soup, right?"

There were so many things on Evergreen Diner's menu that were absolutely delicious, but their California Club and Tomato Soup were in my top five favorites.

I pushed up for another kiss, whispering, "I love you."

When I pulled back, his lips were smiling and his eyes were lit with happiness. "Love you right back, baby. You having a good day so far?"

"So far. How about you?"

"It just got a whole lot better." God, I'd forgotten how damn good he was at lighting me up from the inside. "But I have to admit, I have an ulterior motive," he confessed, his expression growing sheepish. "I've been tryin' my hardest to put Gypsy off on forcin' you and the kids to come for family dinner, but she called today and informed me we'd be having it at our house this weekend. Some bullshit excuse about a busted oven or something, but the truth is, she's run out of patience and is trying to force my hand. I totally understand if it's too soon. If you want, you can take the kids to your mom's for a few hours Sunday night, and I'll make up an excuse for you."

"Or, and I'm just throwing this out there . . . we could stay and have dinner with your family."

I could tell by the way his eyes heated that he really liked that idea. "You sure? I mean, we haven't even talked to the kids about all of this yet. I don't want you to feel pressured into moving faster than you're comfortable with."

Logically, I knew that our relationship was only hours old and other people might look at us and think we were moving too fast—we were already living together, after all—but it felt like the past twenty years didn't exist, that we'd picked up right where we left off before everything had gone south. I was happy for the first time in far too long, and I wasn't going to let anything or anyone dictate the speed of this relationship. That was up to Rhodes and me alone.

"That family dinner is still a few days away, so we have time to figure out how we're going to tell the kids." I reached out and took his hands in mine. "You aren't going to scare me off," I assured him. I knew it was exactly what he needed to hear when his shoulders slumped and his lips pursed on a relieved exhale. "I told you, I'm in this with you, Rhodes. I promise."

He tucked his finger under my chin and guided me forward for another kiss. "Love you, Angel."

My smile was so wide it made my cheeks hurt. "I love you too."

A sexy, gratified sound rumbled up from his chest. "Say it again."

I giggled and shook my head. "I love you too."

"And again."

"Love you."

"Fuck," he rasped. "I'll never get tired of hearing that."

"And I'll never get tired of saying it. But we both need to get back to work." I leaned forward and lowered my voice to a whisper so only he could hear. "I'll gladly say it over and over later tonight while I show you how much I mean it."

The grin that split his face hit me right in the core. He really was the most beautiful man. "I'm holdin' you to that, baby. See you later."

"See you at home."

He glanced back over his shoulder. "Love hearin' you call it home too."

I waited until he walked through the door and disappeared out of view of the windows before turning around, only now remembering I wasn't alone, that a gaggle of nosy women had been standing behind me the entire time. However, the earlier humor was gone from their expressions, and they were looking at me with something I couldn't quite place. That was, until Gretchen spoke.

"I really love this for you, B."

Heather nodded in agreement. "You're so sweet, and we know you've been through a really rough time, so seeing what we just saw . . . well, we're so glad you're happy."

I'd always enjoyed the women I worked with, they were colorful and funny and told it like it was, but I didn't realize until then how much I'd grown to like them. In that moment, I stopped considering them co-workers and started thinking of them as friends. "Thank you," I said past the lump of emotion in my throat. "That really means a lot. The past several months have been difficult, but you should know you guys made them a little bit easier."

Diana rushed forward and wrapped her arms around me, squeezing to the point of crushing my lungs.

"Di?" I wheezed, struggling to pull in a breath. "You okay?"

"You're the nicest person I've ever met. I'm really glad you're happy, is all."

"Well holy crap," Gretchen started dramatically. "Who knew she had any feelings beyond arousal?"

She pulled away, shooting a killing look at Gretchen before batting the dampness from her eyes. "He looks like he knows how to lay pipe," she added in typical Diana fashion, "and if there's a woman who deserves a good railing, it's you."

Heather threw her arms up in defeat. "And there's the real Di," she grumbled as I tossed my head back and laughed, feeling a lightness I hadn't felt in a really long time.

# Chapter Twenty-Four

## Rhodes

I was tucked somewhere between asleep and awake when I registered Blythe's body tensing beside me, but I was slammed right into consciousness when I heard a little voice whisper, "See, I told you Mommy was in here." That sounded like Adeline.

Another voice chimed in, asking, "Why do you think Mom's sleepin' in Rhodes's bed?" That question came from Avett.

"Why isn't he wearin' a shirt?" the tiniest voice of all asked.

*Perfect.* All three of them were here, standing beside the bed their mother and I were lying in.

"'Cause boys don't sleep in shirts, duh," Avett said

like he knew all there was to know when it came to being a boy.

He was right, though. I didn't sleep in shirts. Before they moved in, I didn't sleep in anything at all. But thank Christ I'd broken that habit and at least started wearing underwear. It was for reasons like this right here.

"But Daddy slept in a shirt," Adeline pointed out. "Do you think it was 'cause his tummy was soft and fluffy, and he wanted to hide it like Ms. Deloris at the city pool, who always swam in a T-shirt?"

Blythe's body began to tremble with suppressed laughter as we both struggled to keep up the ruse that we were asleep.

"Rhodes's tummy isn't soft and fluffy," Adeline continued to point out. "It's really bumpy."

"Those are muscles," Avett pointed out. "I'm gonna have muscles like that too when I get big."

"Look," Ainsley squeaked. "He got a drawin' on his booby."

I almost lost it with that one and had to bite down on the inside of my cheek to keep from laughing.

"It's not a booby. It's a pec," Avett said with the kind of disgust that could only come from a big brother. "And that's a tattoo."

"What's a tattoo?"

"It's where they stab ink into your skin with a bunch of needles."

I felt a breath flutter against my skin as one of them came in closer. "It's real pretty." *Ainsley.*

"Don't touch it!" Adeline hissed. I heard a shuffle that must have been her pulling her little sister back from the bed. "You're gonna wake them up."

"But . . . I'm hungry." I could hear the pout in Ainsley's voice. "I wanna wake up Mommy to make me waffles."

"No, don't wake her up," Adeline scolded. "She looks really comfy. And see how Rhodes is huggin' her? I don't think she wants to wake up right now."

My heart clenched, that sweet little girl tugging at its strings and making a place just for her inside of it. To most people she might come off as shy, her quietness mistaken for nerves or trepidation. But I knew the truth. She wasn't shy, she was watchful. She was quiet because that made it easier to soak up everything happening around her. An intuition like hers was going to make her an unstoppable force when she grew up. Hell, I wouldn't be surprised if she ended up as President one day.

"Rhodes gives good hugs. I bet that's why she's in here," Ainsley stated with complete seriousness, carving out a space of her own in my heart.

"Yeah, and he's super cool and smart. I'm gonna be

just like him when I get bigger." Avett declared, taking up his own space.

I felt Blythe's fingers wrap around the forearm I had draped around her waist, squeezing as she listened to her kids give me some of the greatest gifts I'd received, without even realizing they were doing it.

As badly as I wanted to stay in bed all day with Blythe, with three kids under our roof, that wasn't in the cards, and given what they walked in on this morning, I knew the talk we'd been planning was going to have to happen soon. So instead of staying curled around Blythe, I sprang into action.

I shot up to sitting with a roar that made all three of them scream bloody murder, but before they could act, my arms shot out and wrapped around all three of them, scooping them up and dragging them into the bed.

Their screams quickly turned to giggles as I got to work tickling them until they were squirming and flailing everywhere. Blythe quickly got into the game and joined me, acting as a second tickle monster while her kids filled the room with the most beautiful sounds of laughter—when they weren't begging for mercy, of course.

We finally let up when Avett issued the warning that he was about to pee his pants. Their laughter eventually died down, and Adeline crawled over to snuggle up in her mom's lap while Ainsley snuggled into mine. Avett sat in the middle of the bed smiling at the scene in front of him. I knew Blythe wished he was still little enough for snuggles, but he was too focused on growing up and becoming a man, and according to him, men didn't snuggle. I'd been the same at his age. So had my brothers, Raylan and Raleigh. But there would still be days when he needed his momma's arms around him.

Ainsley smiled up at me, her little baby teeth on full display as she said, "I like your toot-toot."

My brows puckered together. "My what?"

She reached over to trace the angel wings on my chest with her tiny finger. "Your toot-toot."

"Oh." My chest shook on a deep chuckle. "My tattoo."

"Dat's what I said." I hugged her tightly, praying she never started saying her Rs and THs correctly.

"Thank you, sweetheart." I glanced over at Blythe to see her watching us with a tender look on her face, those turquoise eyes filled with happiness. "They're actually for your momma."

I could see realization dawning in Avett's eyes. "'Cause you call her Angel."

"That's right, bud. See, your mom and I were really close a long, long time ago, and I never forgot her." I gave the woman who held my heart a soft smile. "She never stopped bein' special to me."

"*I love you*," she mouthed just for me before Adeline chimed in. "That was fun."

"It was, but from here on out, you guys need to knock before you come in Rhodes's room," Blythe said, adopting her mom voice so her kids knew she was serious.

Adeline nodded. "Yes, ma'am. But we only came in 'cause you weren't in your room and we couldn't find you."

Ainsley nodded with a look of seriousness on her face that no four-year-old should have been able to pull off. "Yeah, and that monster in my belly is back, and he's growlin' that he needs waffles."

I adopted her same solemness and said, "You know what? I have a monster in my belly too, and he was demandin' the same thing."

She sucked in a gasp and looked up at me with those wide Caribbean eyes that matched her mother's. "Really?"

I lifted my hand in the air. "Swear. So we better get downstairs and make those waffles."

The three of them bolted off the bed and out of the room, running down the stairs like a herd of elephants.

I slid on a pair of sweats and a T-shirt while Blythe

gathered her hair up in a messy bun on the top of her head. "So . . . I guess the cat's out of the bag on our relationship," I hedged. "But if you aren't ready, we can make an excuse or somethin'. Maybe tell them you had a bad dream—?"

She came over to me and caressed my cheek. "We don't need to make excuses. We're going to tell them the truth."

My heart started racing, the desire for her that was always coursing through my veins pumping even faster. "You sure, baby? I don't want you to feel rushed."

"I love you," she said sincerely. "This isn't rushed. It's time. Now, we better get downstairs fast. If we don't get those waffles cooking, Ainsley's likely to set the kitchen on fire."

We got the waffles made without any risk of devastation, and gathered around the island, the kids tucked up on stools while Blythe and I stood across from them as they stuffed their faces.

My heart lodged in my throat as soon as Blythe started talking. "So, guys, there's something Rhodes and I would like to talk to you about."

"Are you guys boyfriend and girlfriend?" Avett asked around a mouthful of waffle, his cheeks puffed out like a chipmunk storing up food for the winter. "Is that why you were huggin' Momma in your bed?"

I looked to her for guidance, returning the small, almost secretive grin. "Yeah, buddy," she answered, turning back to face the kids that had come to mean everything to me. "Actually, if you ever wake up and need to find me, you can find me in there. Rhodes and I share that room now."

"'Cause he makes you happy?" I felt Avett's question like a blow to the chest, and I felt Blythe's answer the same.

"Exactly. Because he makes me happy. Just like you guys make me happy."

I couldn't keep quiet any longer, I needed them to know what they meant to me. All of them. "Your mom makes me happy too," I told them. "But I really lucked out, because she comes with you, and you guys make me just as happy as your mom does."

Adeline's eyes glistened. Avett's chest swelled up and his throat worked. And Ainsley grinned like I just told her she was actually born a princess.

"I love your mom very much. And I want you to know that I love all of you too. Just as much. And I want you guys to stay here with me forever. I want this to be your home."

"We can stay here forever?" Ainsley bounced on her stool excitedly and squeaked, "Does that mean we can get horses?"

"Ains. You can't just ask someone—"

I cut Blythe off. "You want a horse, baby girl, I'll get you a horse." Blythe whipped her head in my direction, bugging her eyes out in shock. But I wasn't taking it back. I was actually excited at the prospect of spoiling those kids rotten. There wasn't anything I wouldn't do or give to make them happy.

She'd simply have to learn to accept that. Because I had every intention of spoiling her rotten too.

We finished breakfast and were in the middle of rinsing dishes when Avett spoke. "Just so you know, we love you too," he informed me. His words froze me in place.

Adeline came up beside him and nodded sagely. "We do. Even if you don't buy us a horse."

Hell, I'd get them ten fucking horses each.

Blythe let out a giggle and shook her head, grinning so brightly it lit up the whole house. "You are so screwed."

I was. And I didn't give a single damn.

# Chapter Twenty-Five

## Blythe

Nerves danced beneath my skin like a million ants crawling all over me. I spun around in front of the bathroom mirror, taking my outfit in from all angles. Like the seven others I'd tried on before, it didn't feel right.

"Damn it," I grumbled, reaching for the hem of the dress and yanking it up over my head, leaving me in only my panties and bra.

Rhodes came sauntering into the bathroom, dressed in his usual jeans, cotton tee, and motorcycle boots like it was just any other day. I caught his smirk in the mirror before spinning around and stomping back to the massive closet we now shared, flipping through hangers frantically, like I didn't already know exactly what I had.

"What was wrong with that one?"

"It was too casual," I muttered.

He stepped into the doorway of the closet. "Baby, it's just dinner. It's meant to be casual."

I spun around and planted my hands on my hips, shooting him a look that never failed to send my kids running off to do whatever I'd ordered. "It's *family* dinner," I stressed.

His brow furrowed as he leaned his shoulder against the frame and crossed his arms over his chest. "You're actin' like you don't already know them. We practically grew up together, Blythe. You're just as much family in their eyes as I am. Hell, probably more so, given what day it is."

I knew I wasn't acting rationally, but I couldn't seem to get my bearings. I'd never been worried about impressing Elliott's family. They'd been different. Less affectionate and more formal, so I never got too close to any of them. Rhodes's family was different. When we were together as kids, they'd taken me into the fold. I was an honorary Bradbury. I knew they still cared about me, that I was important to them, but this felt different. I wasn't having a casual dinner with them as Sunny's best friend. I was having dinner with them tonight as Rhodes's girlfriend. The woman he'd be spending the rest of his life with. The woman who was bringing three children to the table with her. This wasn't casual for me. I intended to make a statement tonight. And that statement was that I was here for good. This was it. I wasn't thinking rings or wedding bells, mainly because I didn't need any of that to be happy with Rhodes. But still, I wasn't going anywhere ever again. "I don't want them to think I'm not taking this seriously."

He pushed off the door jamb and moved closer, reaching out to caress my upper arms. "Baby, they aren't comin' here tonight with any expectations other than eating good food and bein' in good company."

"Shit . . . the roast!" I blurted, making a move for the open closet door. The last thing I needed when I was this damn nervous was to burn the main entrée.

Rhodes grabbed my arm before I could bolt out of the closet, using my own momentum to whip me around. "I already took it out. Everything's fine."

My chest heaved on a sigh of relief. That was one box checked. Now if I could find something to wear . . .

Rhodes dragged his hand down my arms and rested his palms on my hips as his amber eyes skated up and down my barely-clothed body. "You know, I think I have just the cure for your nerves," he rumbled as he slowly backed me deeper into the closet.

Goosebumps spread across my skin at the feral expression on his face, my core clenching and my nipples tightening beneath my bra. "Oh?" My tongue darted out to swipe across my bottom lip. "And what would that be?"

His grin was positively devilish as he toyed with the strings at my hips, pulling the material tighter and tighter, until it was at risk of snapping. "Droppin' down to my knees and fuckin' you with my tongue till you come all over my face."

My pussy spasmed, silently begging for exactly that. My chest wobbled on a shaky inhale as I cast a glance over his shoulder. "The kids," I said in a weak attempt at an objection.

"They're all downstairs, currently occupied with things that'll keep them down there for at least another ten minutes. I already locked the door, and if I can't make you come in ten minutes, I'm fallin' down on the job as your man." He leaned forward, dragging his nose along the side of mine. "What do you say, Angel? You gonna let me have my dessert before dinner? Because my mouth is already watering for you."

I blinked up at him through the fan of my eyelashes, a wicked grin stretching across my face as I placed my hands on his shoulders and applied pressure. "Get on your knees for me like a good boy and I'll give you your reward."

The sound he made was positively primitive as he lowered to the floor in front of me. His expression turned ravenous as he yanked my panties down my hips, tapping one ankle, then the other, in silent command for me to step out of them. As soon as I did, he scooped up the scrap of silk and lace and stuffed it into his back pocket, and I knew without a doubt that I was never getting those panties back.

His nose bumped against my clit as he leaned forward and inhaled deeply, pulling the scent of my arousal into his lungs and drawing a gasp from my chest.

He grabbed my right leg and hiked my thigh over his shoulder, opening me up to him and letting out a pleased hum at what he saw. "Already dripping for me." His eyes traveled up my body and latched onto mine. Does having me on my knees turn you on, Blythe?"

"More than you could possibly imagine—" My words cut off with a sharp cry when his tongue darted out and slid through my wet, swollen folds, from my entrance to my clit.

Rhodes's growl vibrated against my core, shooting sparks of electricity through my body. "Your taste is the only thing I've ever craved," he grunted before spearing his tongue inside me. "Could spend the rest of my life feastin' on only you and live the very best life a man could live."

"Rhodes," I panted and my fingers tangled in his hair, holding him in place as my hips began to circle, chasing after his tongue. I grew more desperate for my release by the second, every muscle and fiber in my body stringing tighter. I rode his face with abandon, my moans and whimpers growing louder and more frantic as he alternated between fucking me with his tongue and sucking on my clit.

"More, baby," I pleaded, feeling like I was standing on the edge of the abyss, desperately waiting to be pushed over into nothingness. "*Please.*"

Just like that, he plunged two fingers as deep inside me as they could go and curled them forward, stroking against that spot inside me that had me seeing stars. When his lips surrounded my clit and sucked, I went off. Stars burst in front of my eyes, and I tipped right over the edge, my mouth open on a silent scream as wave after wave washed over me.

Just before the one knee I still had holding me up could give out, Rhodes stood to his full height and held me up. Something told me he would always be there to catch me before I could fall. And I would try my hardest to do the very same for him.

He smiled rakishly, licking my arousal off his lips.

"Three minutes," he said triumphantly. "Looks like we have a few more minutes to spare."

I reached down and made quick work of popping the button on his jeans and yanking down the zipper. I pulled my bottom lip between my teeth and bit down as I slipped my hand inside his boxer briefs and fisted his cock.

"Then I guess you better hurry up and fuck me before the clock runs out."

Rhodes hoisted me up by the backs of my knees, wrapping my legs around his waist and walking me back until my back hit the wall. My nails dug into his shoulders and I cried out as he drove his cock into me from the root in one quick, brutal thrust.

"*Fuck*," he barked out, pausing long enough for us both to adjust. Me to being so full and him to being squeezed to death by my pussy. He braced one arm beneath my ass to keep me in place while he lifted the other hand and collared his fingers around my throat, applying the lightest, most delicious pressure as his thumb tilted my chin up so I could drown in his eyes.

"Gonna spend the rest of my life fuckin' you like this," he grunted, his hips slamming against me as he powered in and out of me, his cock driving at an almost brutal pace. "I'll wake up and fuck you like this. Go to bed at night and do it all over again. I'll gladly leave this earth with my cock buried so deep inside you I don't know where I end and you begin. There won't be a day that comes I don't tell you I love you. But this . . ." He slammed into me again, the base of his shaft rubbing against my swollen clit as he circled his hips, reaching a place inside me no one ever had before.

"Baby," I said on a whine, the pressure building so high it almost scared me.

"This is how I'll show you. Every. Fuckin'. *Day*." He punctuated each of those words with a thrust, and on the last one, something inside me detonated.

He followed after me a moment later, burying himself deep and pressing against me as he groaned into my neck while emptying himself inside me.

When we both finally managed to catch our breath, he pulled back to look down at me, brushing the hair back from my forehead with the hand that I'd been wearing as a necklace.

I smiled at him and leaned in to press a kiss to his lips. "I can't think of a better way to spend ten minutes."

Then we both burst into laughter.

Koda let out a happy bark at the sound of the doorbell, like she already knew who was standing on the front porch.

My heart did a little skip as I smoothed the front of my dress for the millionth time. Rhodes had been right. He'd managed to make me forget all about my nerves, but now that the time had come, they were back with a vengeance.

"I'll get it!" Avett shouted, skidding around the stairs on his socked feet. Before he could make it, though, Rhodes was there, placing a hand on the top of his head to stop him.

"Sorry, buddy. You have a few more years before you're the one who can answer the door."

"But—"

He gave his head a formal shake. "No 'buts', buddy. It's not about you bein' little or grown. It's about safety. I take your safety very seriously. Yours and your mom's and sisters'. Far as I'm concerned, it's my responsibility, so until your momma and I say it's time, you wait for one us to answer the door." Rhodes held his hand out to my son. "Understood?"

Avett took his hand, his face growing serious as he shook it. "Understood."

Rhodes grinned and ruffled his hair again. When he

murmured "Good man," Avett's chest swelled so big it was a wonder it didn't pop.

With that handled—and so brilliantly—he moved past me, pausing long enough to press a kiss to my lips and whisper, "Most beautiful woman in the whole world." Then he passed by to let his family into our home.

*Our home.*

The second he twisted the knob, the door burst open so fast I thought for a second it was going to take Rhodes to the ground. He managed to keep his feet under him, but I barely had time to feel relief before three familiar faces came rushing at me like they hadn't seen me in decades.

"You're finally here!" Gypsy cried, throwing her arms wide and wrapping them around my neck as soon as she collided with me. Sunny was next, followed by their youngest sister, Holly. The three of them wrapped me in an embrace full of so much love it nearly choked me.

"Hi," I croaked, doing my best to get my arms around the three of them. Over their shoulders, I saw Marco, Raylan, Raleigh, and Aaron come through the door and lifted my hand in a wave. They chuckled and returned it.

"I can't tell you how happy it makes me that you're

back with my brother," Sunny said tearfully. "My bestie is finally going to become my sister!"

"Yeah. Now that you're back we finally have a shot at not being outnumbered by testosterone."

I giggled just as Gypsy reached up and cupped my cheeks in both hands. Her eyes shone with happy tears.

"I'm so glad you're finally home, sweetheart." She cast a look at her oldest brother and smiled. "It's been far too long. For the both of you."

# Chapter Twenty-Six

## Blythe

It had been three weeks since the dinner with Rhodes's family, and the only way I knew to describe how it had been was bliss.

Pure and simple bliss.

I was letting go of the past and keeping my eyes on the future, and I was happier than I could remember being in a very long time. My kids were living their best lives, work was good, I was reconnecting with old friends and making new ones, and I was mending the bonds with my own family after being away for too long. Life was good.

There was just one dark cloud hanging over top of it. And that dark cloud came in the form of a beautiful dark-haired woman with sad eyes who did everything she could to hide herself away from the world while still being forced to exist in it.

Seeing her shrink into herself more and more as the days turned into weeks broke my heart. I would have given anything to be able to help her, but I didn't know how to get her to open up to me, to ask for help. I'd done everything I could think of, but I was all out of ideas.

The woman in question stood from her chair at the station beside mine and headed out of our little nook. I couldn't help but notice she was moving gingerly, her motions slower and more careful than usual.

I turned in my chair, my gaze tracking her as she disappeared from sight.

"Keep trying." Gretchen's voice broke through the cloud of worry in my head, and I twisted around to look at her. She tilted her chin in the direction Merritt had just disappeared. "We've seen you trying to break through. If there's anyone here who can, it's you."

"Do you know what's going on with her?"

She shook her head. "None of us ever got close enough to find out. At first we thought she was shy, but now we're not so sure."

I didn't feel I had either, but I'd been paying closer attention than most might have. "I think it's him," I said quietly.

Gretchen's eyes widened and she lowered her voice,

glancing around to make sure no one could overhear. "Him, as in her husband?" I nodded.

"What do you think is going on?"

It wasn't so much me thinking any longer; I'd seen enough signs to be confident now. "He's beating her. I'd bet my life on it." As I said those words, the anger in my belly built to a boil, and I wanted nothing more than to track him down and give him the same treatment he'd given to his wife who was so much smaller than he was.

"Damn it," Gretchen hissed, slapping her hand against her thigh. "I should have known. That son of a bitch was too damn charming, should have seen that as a sign."

"They're master manipulators for a reason, Gretch. Don't beat yourself up. Most people wouldn't have put it together. That's how they're able to get away with it for so long."

"Yeah, but you did."

I pushed to my feet. "Unfortunately, I learned from the manipulator I was married to. I just didn't realize the truth until he was gone."

With that, I moved out of the office area in search of Merritt. She wasn't in the break room, so I continued down the hall to the ladies room at the very end. I heard it as soon as I pushed the door open. The quiet sniffle and the muted sob she was struggling to hold in. The sound of her crying killed me, and I decided then and there I was done waiting for her to reach out on her own.

"I'm not going anywhere," I said, mindful to keep my voice gentle. "So there's no use trying to hide from me in there."

I waited patiently as silence filled the bathroom; finally, a full minute later, the lock on the stall door clicked and it swung open. Merritt stepped out, her eyes red and puffy from crying.

"Oh, honey," I breathed, my eyes beginning to burn as I stepped closer. "How can I help?"

She pulled in a broken breath. "I—I need help wrapping my ribs. I can't get the bandage myself, and it's getting harder to breathe."

I nodded, unable to speak past the lump in my throat. I blinked rapidly and had to bite the inside of my cheek until I tasted blood to fight back the tears as she lifted the top of her scrubs, revealing the ugly, mottled blue and purple bruises that covered her entire left side. If she was asking for help with something like this, I couldn't imagine the kind of pain she'd been suffering all morning.

I held out my hand, taking the wrap from her, unable to stop the one tear that broke free and slipped down my cheek.

"It's not as bad as it looks, honestly," she attempted

to assure me. "Sometimes I'm too clumsy for my own good." She attempted to laugh but cut it off with a wince when the movement jostled her battered ribs. I knew this wasn't something she'd done to herself. As I wrapped the bandage around her, there was no mistaking the bruise was shaped like the sole of a shoe down near her hip.

"You shouldn't have come in today, honey. You need to be in bed resting."

"Best way to deal with pain is to work through it." Her eyes were hollow as she stared straight ahead, and I knew those words weren't her own. That piece of shit had beaten her to the point she struggled to breathe, then he'd forced her to come to work while she still wore the proof of his temper all over her body.

"Merritt." My voice came out in a croak as I moved to stand in front of her and placed my hands on her shoulders. "Please, let me help you. *Please.*"

"There's nothing to help with. I told you, I was clumsy, and I slipped at the top of the stairs."

I shook my head, silently communicating that I wasn't going to accept her lie as truth. "You don't deserve this."

Her chin began to tremble as she bit down on her bottom lip. "Maybe I do," she whispered.

"No," I argued vehemently. "No, you don't. That's

him making you think that. He's trying to convince you that everything he's done is a lesson you need to learn, that you're defective and don't deserve better. *He's* the defective one, and he knows it. That's why he's doing this. He's trying to beat you down and make you believe you're lucky to have him because he knows you could do so much better. But more, he knows that he can't. You're the prize, Merritt. *You*."

"You—you don't understand."

"Then help me to," I pleaded, hopelessness making my chest heavy.

"He won't let me go," she confessed, her voice breaking. "I've tried to leave, but he won't let me go."

I was going to kill this asshole if I ever got my hands on him. But first, I was going to help Merritt get out from under his thumb.

"I know people who can help," I insisted. "My brother, he's a detective with the Hope Valley PD."

Her eyes went wide, filling with panic as she shook her head frantically. "No, you can't do that. You don't understand. He's powerful. He has connections. The police can't do anything."

I had a feeling Tristan wouldn't be too happy to hear that his hands were tied in any situation of wrong-doing. He'd become a cop because of what we went through as kids. It had cultivated a deep-seated need to help other people inside him. To his core, he was a protector, and he wouldn't stand for anyone, powerful or not, hurting someone else.

But that was a conversation for another time.

For now, there *was* somebody who could help. Someone who didn't have the same red tape to cut through or rules to follow.

"Okay. No police," I assured her. "But there are still options. Have you heard of Alpha Omega?"

I knew she had by the look that flashed over her face. "I can't afford—"

I cut her off by shaking my head. "Don't even think about that. Something you might not know about those men; money doesn't matter to them when a wrong is being done. And I know this for a fact, because the man I love is one of them, and he would bend over backward and work himself to the bone to help someone who truly needed it. All without ever taking a single penny. It's why I love him."

"That man who came in here a couple months back?"

I smiled and nodded. "Yeah. Him. He can help you, Merritt. And he'll gladly do it because he cares and it's important to him. But what's more, he knows you're important to me."

A sob broke past her lips as her knees gave out, and I

moved in quickly, catching her before she hit the ground while trying to make sure I didn't hurt her worse than she already was.

"Shh," I soothed, rubbing a hand over her hair. "You're going to be okay. I give you my word."

"I-I've never been important to anybody."

I wasn't sure my heart could take much more, but I'd do my best to deal, for her, because Lord knew she'd already suffered more than I could ever comprehend. "You do now. And something you need to know about me . . . when someone is important to me, there isn't anything I won't do for them." I waited until she was stable on her feet before pulling back so she could see my face. "You take care of what you need to in here, and I'm going to go start my car. Then I'm taking you to see the people who can help."

I began to turn, but Merritt stopped me by grabbing my hand. "Thank you," she said quietly. "I don't think I'll ever be able to repay you for this."

I shook my head and caressed her cheek. "That's another thing, Merritt, friends don't pay friends back for caring. Don't start a running tally, because I'll never cash it in." I swiped her tear away and smiled. "See you out there."

She nodded and I left the bathroom, swinging by to grab my purse and ask Gretchen if she could cover the front for a couple hours, then I headed out back to my car.

I fished around in my purse for my keys, finally finding them at the bottom of my bag. Pushing the button on the key fob, I beeped the locks and opened the driver's side door as an angry voice spoke behind me.

"Fuckin' bitch. It's time someone teaches you your place, and I'm looking forward to doing it." I barely made it halfway around when something slammed into my temple so hard spots formed before my eyes as my legs crumpled beneath me. Then all I saw was darkness.

# Chapter Twenty-Seven

## Rhodes

"What do you think about this one? It looks nice."

I moved over to the case Tristan was standing in front of and bent to get a better look at the ring he was pointing at. When I decided it was time to go ring shopping for Blythe, I knew I wanted her brother to come with me. They shared a special bond no other siblings could understand unless they'd gone through something traumatic together. I knew that from experience with my brothers and sisters as well.

He and Blythe were so close, I knew he'd have a good idea of what she would like. Everything he'd suggested would have worked great. But something didn't feel right about any of them.

"Nah. That's not it."

He let out a grunted curse. "That's what you've said about every one so far."

And I would continue to say it until I found the perfect ring. None of the ones I'd seen were Blythe. She needed something more than a simple ring. She deserved something special. Something you wouldn't see on another person.

The jeweler came over. "Maybe if you tell me a little about her, I could help point you in the right direction."

"She's fierce and protective. Her three kids are the most important things in her whole world, and the four of them are the most important things in mine. She has eyes the color of the Caribbean on a warm, sunny day. And every time I look into them, I think how happy I'd be to drown right there."

"This is starting to feel a little uncomfortable for me," Tristan grunted, but I ignored him, focused on the task at hand.

"I've loved her since I was seventeen years old, more than half my life, and I'll continue loving her, even when I'm no longer on this earth."

The older man hummed, tapping his chin as he scanned the rows of cases in the store. He was silent for so long I started to feel like I was coming out of my skin.

Then his eyes lit up and he snapped his fingers. "I think I might have the perfect ring."

We followed him toward a case at the back of the store. "Now, I didn't suggest looking here, because these aren't complete sets, but if you'll bear with me, I have an idea."

He slid the glass panel aside at the back of the case and reached in, plucking a ring from one of the cushions and bringing it out, holding it up for us to inspect. The moment I laid eyes on it, my heart kicked into a gallop, and I knew. Around the prongs for a center stone were four small round diamonds. One for me, Avett, Adeline, and Ainsley. The band was a shiny white gold, solid and strong, lined all the way around with much smaller diamonds. Everything about it screamed Blythe.

"I know it's hard to picture without the two karat center stone in place. Most people would go the traditional route with another diamond, but based on your description, I was thinking she might appreciate something a bit more creative, say, blue topaz."

I lifted my gaze to the man who was smiling brightly. "Some say blue topaz looks a lot like the Caribbean Ocean on a summer day. I don't believe that's a coincidence."

I didn't either. This was the ring meant to be on her finger.

Tristan clapped me on the shoulder, giving me a little jostle. "She's gonna love that, brother."

"I'll take it. With the blue topaz in the center."

He dipped his head in a nod. "Of course, sir. I'll get to work setting that personally. It'll take me a few days, but I promise it'll be worth it."

I had no doubt.

The clerk rang me up, and Tristan and I were heading out when my cell started to ring. Pulling it from my pocket, I swiped across the screen and brought it to my ear, answering, "Bradbury."

"Rhodes, it's Linc. How fast do you think you can get back to the office?"

My back shot straight, a chill skating across my shoulders and down my spine. "Maybe ten minutes. Why? What's goin' on?"

"Need you to get back here as fast as you can, son. It's about Blythe."

I was running to my truck before he finished his sentence. Tristan was already on my tail when I clipped, "We gotta move. Let's go."

"What's goin' on?" he asked as he pulled himself up into the passenger seat.

I threw the truck into gear and slammed on the gas pedal. "Not sure. But Linc said to get back to AO fast. That it has somethin' to do with Blythe."

"Fuck," Tristan hissed beside me, raking his fingers through his hair, the agitation suddenly rolling off him matching the turmoil currently swirling around in my chest.

"What's goin' on?" I barked as soon as I pushed through the door into the lobby.

Lincoln was already there, prepared for me to barrel in like a freight train. "My office," he said before turning to Tristan. "Son, maybe it would be best if you headed on home—"

"All due respect, Lincoln . . . but fuck that. This is my sister. If she's involved, so am I."

With that, both of us pushed through the lobby and into Linc's office where a few more of the Alpha Omega guys stood, along with a woman I recalled seeing when I took lunch to Blythe at her work, though I couldn't recall her name.

"Fill me in. What's happening?"

Blythe's co-worker pushed to the center of the room. Her face was white as a sheet and she was wringing her fingers together so tight in front of her, I worried she might hurt herself.

"Um, I'm Merritt. I work with Blythe. We're . . . friends," she explained, that last word coming from her lips like she wasn't familiar with using it. "There was a situation at work today, and she wanted to bring me here so you could help—" She cut herself off, her eyes darted around the room nervously as she licked her lips and pulled her bottom lip between her teeth. Whatever she needed to say, it was clearly hard for her, but I could see the fight in her eyes. "She found out my husband's been hitting me, and she wanted to help," she rushed out, her cheeks flushing a bright pink as tears welled up in her eyes.

"She told me if there was anyone who could help, it was you guys, and she wanted to bring me over here to talk to you. I was supposed to meet her in the parking lot, but when I got to her car, she wasn't there. I thought maybe I heard her wrong, and she wanted me to meet her here, so I came over. Only . . ." Her nails dug into the heels of her palms hard enough to leave crescent marks in her skin.

Tristan moved before I could process what was happening, stepping forward and gently grabbing hold on her hands, using his thumb to straighten her fingers, preventing her from causing any more damage.

"It's okay," he said in a low, soft tone I'd never heard

him use before. "You're safe here. Take a breath and tell us the rest."

Merritt blinked up at him, and whatever she saw in his gaze had her shoulders squaring and her chin lifting in determination. "I asked Mr. Sheppard if she was here, but he didn't know what I was talking about. I'm worried . . . I think something might have happened to her."

I stepped forward, struggling to keep my voice neutral when it felt like a storm was raging inside me. "Why do you think something happened?"

"Because when I was looking around for her, I saw this old, beat up car turning out of the lot and gunning it down the street. I didn't think anything of it at first." Her chin began to tremble and her eyes welled up. "This is my fault. I should have known."

"No, it's not," Tristan insisted. "You did everything right. You came here and you told Linc, and because of that, we're gonna find her."

"Are you . . . are you Tristan?" she asked quietly.

He nodded. "I am. Blythe's my sister, and we're going to get her back."

"You promise?"

"I swear."

Everything moved at lightning speed then. Tristan

had no choice but to call Nona and Trick and tell them what was happening. School would be letting out soon, and I needed someone I could trust to get the kids so I could do everything in my power to make sure I brought their mother home.

Nona assured me she would keep them safe, while Trick insisted on coming into the office to help in any way he could.

Thanks to Merritt's description, we knew the make and model of the car we suspected took off with Blythe inside. Our tech guy, Tony, got busy hacking into the security cameras all around the parking lot, scrolling through hours of footage for the car.

"Got something," he called from behind a wall of monitors. Tristan and I ran over, leaning in to watch the screen he pointed to. "I got the car pulling into the parking lot a little after nine this morning. Whoever was inside didn't get out. They sat there for the next three hours, staking the place out." He hit a button to speed through the footage, slowing it again when it showed Blythe exit the back of the building.

My heart lurched painfully as I watched the woman I loved on the grainy screen. She wasn't paying attention to her surroundings as she dug around in her purse for her keys. I decided right then and there that we were going to have a fight about this once I got her home safely. Because I was absolutely going to find her, and she was going to be okay. There was no other acceptable outcome. I'd lived without her for twenty years, and I refused to live another minute of another day without her.

On the screen, a man dressed in dark clothes rushed her from behind. He must have said something because she started to turn, but before she could get a look at him, he pulled a gun from the pocket of his hoodie and slammed the butt of it into her temple.

Bile crawled up my throat as I watched her crumple to the ground, then the asshole who was as good as dead dragged her back to his car, dumping her limp body into the back seat of his piece of shit car, and took off.

"Do we have another angle where we can see his face, or even the plates on his car?"

Tony's fingers flew over the keyboard in a blur, and a minute later we were watching the same footage from a different camera.

"That motherfucker," I hissed, rage and adrenaline dumping into my blood and making my vision go red.

"You know that guy?" Linc asked from his place behind me.

"That's Lonny *fuckin'* Oswald."

Tristan's head whipped around in my direction.

"That piece of shit from high school who used to call you Trashbury?"

I nodded as my fingers clenched into fists and my molars ground together. "That's him."

"What reason could he possibly have for attacking and abducting Blythe?"

"Pride," I grunted. "He pulled his shit at The Tap Room a couple months back, and your sister put him in his place."

Tristan stood tall, slowly pivoting to face me. "Meaning?"

"Meaning, when he wouldn't take a hint, she insulted him. Then when he started hurling insults my way because she'd bruised his ego, your sister punched him in the throat in front of the entire goddamn bar."

Tristan raked his hands through his hair in frustration. "Jesus Christ. She's always been too damn protective of the people she cares about."

"Well that's a lecture you can dish out once we find her. Tony, pull up anything and everything you can find on Lonny Oswald. We're gonna need property records, last known address—"

My phone buzzed in my pocket as I rattled off instructions, but time slowed to a crawl when I pulled it out and saw the alert on the screen. Despite the hurricane swirling around inside me, my lips pulled into a grin as I clicked on the message and pulled up the map.

"Scratch that. I need a team to go in less than two minutes. I know where they are."

Tristan shot me a bewildered look. "How?"

I twisted my phone so he could see the screen. "Because your sister just shared her location with me."

# Chapter Twenty-Eight

Blythe

My head felt like it had been cracked clean in half as my eyelids fluttered, trying to peel open. My stomach rolled violently, and I had to breathe slowly through my nose for several seconds to keep from throwing up.

It took several more seconds for me to understand why whatever I was lying on vibrated beneath me. When my vision finally cleared, I realized I was lying across the back seat of a car that had seen much better days. It smelled like old take-out, sweat, and body odor, and the floor of the back seat was littered with what looked like three weeks' worth of drive-thru trash.

I pushed the remaining nausea, the stabbing pain that started in my temple and radiated through my skull, and the panic clutching at my chest to the back of my mind so I could take stock of everything around me.

"Fuckin' bitch," I heard muttered from the front seat. "Stupid fuckin' cunt. Thinks she's better than me. I'll show her. Won't look better once I'm done with you, bitch."

I held my breath and lifted my head enough to see between the front seats to the man behind the wheel. The voice was familiar, but I still felt a little fuzzy from the blow, so it took a moment to realize it was Lonny Oswald driving the piece-of-shit car I was in.

I bit down on my lips hard enough to taste blood to keep from crying out when he hit a pothole, causing me to bang into the door panel. I lifted my hands, trying to brace myself, only to discover the son of a bitch had bound them in front of me with zip ties.

*Calm down, Blythe,* I told myself when my eyes began to burn with tears and my panic started to grow. *Calm down. You can get out of this. Take a moment and think.*

Closing my eyes, I pulled in a centering breath and pictured my kids' faces in the back of my mind. I thought about how good it felt to wake up every morning wrapped in Rhodes's arms. How much I loved waffle breakfasts with my family. I thought about every single thing that had filled me with happiness recently, and I held those memories close, letting them fill me with strength. I'd been through hell and back, and I'd finally made it to the other side. I wasn't going to let that motherfucker steal my happiness. People like him only wanted to destroy. Their lives were so small and miserable they couldn't stand seeing other people happy. He didn't deserve to win, and I wasn't going to let him.

Panic loosened its hold on me, giving way to a fueling rage. I was getting out of this, one way or another. And when I did, I was going to beat the everloving shit out of Lonny *fucking* Oswald.

I just had to figure out how to do that.

Scanning the floor once again, I spotted my purse tossed among the garbage. I couldn't help but smile as I carefully reached for it, digging inside as quietly as possible for my phone.

If there was one thing you could count on with Lonny, it was that he was as stupid as he looked, which was really saying something, because that prick looked like he'd fallen from the top of the stupid tree and hit every freaking branch on the way down.

I flipped the button to silent as soon as I found it and swiped the screen, bringing it to life, then navigated my way through my texts until I found Rhodes's name. I quickly tapped through the options until I found what I was looking for, and quickly shared my location with him. I waited and prayed he would know what to do.

Ten seconds later my phone lit up with a message.

I see you, Angel. I'm on my way. Stay
safe a little longer.

A single tear broke free as I re-read the message. Because I believed him. He was coming for me, and I had faith he'd make it in time.

For the next ten minutes, I lay there, trying to be as still as possible while I was forced to listen to Lonny curse me under his breath between Kiss and Mötley Crüe songs, making every threat known to man and detailing all the ways he wanted to make me pay for humiliating him.

I wasn't sure which was worse, having to listen to Lonny plot his revenge, or the eighties hair bands he had playing on repeat.

I didn't know where the hell he was taking me, or where we even were, but I hoped I'd gained conscious-ness soon enough that we weren't too far away, because if I had to listen to Gene Simmons sing about how he was made for loving me, or Vince Neal wail "Girls, Girls, Girls," I was going to have to use one of the fast food straws to puncture my eardrums.

I knew the instant Rhodes arrived on the scene,

because the car began to decelerate as Lonny took his foot off the gas to stare out the driver's side window in shock. "What? No! How did that fucker—?"

He twisted and looked back over his shoulder too fast for me to close my eyes in time. "You stupid bitch!" he shrieked.

I kicked out between the seats, my foot bashing against his face. He jerked the wheel as his head slammed into the window from the force, and I nearly rolled off the seat as he over-corrected, sending us swerving all over the road. I managed to keep my balance somehow, and shot up to sitting as he reached for something in the passenger seat. "I'm gonna kill you!" he shouted. Sunlight bounced off the metal of the gun in his hand as he lifted it up and twisted, trying to point it back at me. I lunged forward, grabbing hold of his arm and slamming it against the side of his seat, the force making it bend in a way an arm wasn't supposed to bend.

He let out a high-pitched scream of agony and dropped the gun, but I held onto his arm with a death grip, refusing to let go while I was tossed all around the back seat like a ragdoll as Lonny lost control of the car.

I briefly thought we were going to crash, but I didn't care. Crashing this shitty car was far more preferable to being shot or any of the other things he'd muttered about doing to me.

A flash of silver caught my eye, and I turned in time to see Rhodes's truck pull up alongside us before Lonny wrenched the wheel to the left and Rhodes had to slam on the brakes to avoid being hit or hitting me.

"Let go!" Lonny shrieked. "Let go, let go! You fuckin' bitch!"

I let go, but only because that arm was utterly useless, and I needed my hands free so I could loop them over the headrest and pin him to his seat. "Hit the brakes, you asshole!"

He did as I ordered, slamming on them a little too hard and sending us careening into the ditch on the side of the road. I closed my eyes, shot up a silent prayer to whatever higher power might have been listening to get me out of this alive, and braced myself.

The car bounced violently over the uneven ground before finally lurching to a stop with its nose pointed toward the ground at an angle cars weren't meant to point.

The sound of Lonny sputtering and gagging from my zip ties digging into his neck brought me back to the present and alerted me to the fact that we were both still alive, and at least marginally safe.

Then I remembered what he did and how pissed I was.

"Who's gonna kill who now, motherfucker?" I shouted as my vision washed over with red. I braced my foot in the back of his seat and used it as leverage, pushing off so my bound hands choked him even harder. He thrashed in his seat, unable to get free or reach me with his busted arm.

I was so lost in the wave of violence that had washed over me I hadn't realized my door had been thrown open until I felt a set of hands on me. "No!" I shouted at the person tugging at me. "Let me go! I'm not moving until this piece of shit stops breathing!"

"Angel, it's me." I barely registered Rhodes's voice through my haze of vengeance. "It's me, baby. I'm here. I'm right here."

He finally broke through, and I twisted my head to see the most beautiful sight right there beside me. I let out a sigh of relief, but I didn't loosen my hold on the son of a bitch in the front seat. "You made it," I breathed.

"Told you I would, Angel. And I'll always keep a promise to you."

I smiled. I hadn't thought it possible to love this man any more than I already did, but when he said something like that, I fell all over again. "I knew you would."

"Come on, Blythe. Let's get you out of here, yeah?"

Lonny sputtered and gagged, his one good arm slapping all around, trying to get free. "Not yet," I growled through clenched teeth. "He's still breathing."

"Baby," Rhodes said soothingly. "I understand exactly how you feel. But trust me, it'll feel so much better to know this fucker is rotting in a prison cell every day for the rest of his miserable life than for him to be rotting in the ground where he'll never feel it again."

That did it. I loosened my hold on Lonny's neck and lifted my arms over the back of the seat as he coughed and sputtered. His door flew open and my brother reached in, yanking him out and throwing him on the ground. As Tristan wrenched Lonny's arms behind his back, setting off another series of screams as he cuffed him, I let Rhodes help me out of that God-forsaken car and extended my arms toward him.

"Get these off me," I whispered. "Please, just get them off."

"I got you, baby," he assured me, pulling a pocket knife from his back pocket and slicing through the thick plastic. As soon as he cut me loose, I collapsed into him, wrapping my arms around his neck, and finally allowed myself to break down as he held me up, offering all the support I needed. Just like I knew he always would.

I SAT on the porch swing, rocking back and forth lazily, watching my kids squeal and laugh as they ran through the sprinklers Rhodes set up out back. Koda barked and danced after them, barely dodging the stream in time.

It had been a week since Lonny tried taking his revenge—and in true Lonny fashion, failed epically—and I was finally back to a hundred percent. I'd come out of that ordeal with a couple scrapes and bruises and a pretty nasty concussion, but Lonny had faired much worse. I managed to break his arm in two places and fucked his larynx up enough it required medical attention. He spent two days cuffed to a hospital bed before he was carted off to jail to await arraignment for what he did to me. He was going to prison for a very long time, and I hoped each day was worse than the one before.

Rhodes told me it had been Merritt who alerted them that something was wrong. I'd wanted to see her right away, but I didn't want to risk going to her house and setting off her husband. When I said as much to Rhodes, he informed me things had been set in motion that day. He wouldn't tell me any more since it was officially a case for Alpha Omega, but he assured me she was getting help and asked me to be patient.

That wasn't something I was particularly known for, but I would give it to him. Besides, my time off was finally coming to an end on Monday, so I'd be able to catch up with her and thank her for saving me as soon as I returned to work.

"Hey, Angel," Rhodes said, his voice pulling me from my thoughts and back to the here and now. "You good?"

I smiled, scooting over on the swing so he could sit beside me. As soon as his arm looped around my shoulders, I nuzzled into his side, contentment washing over me. "Baby, I'm fantastic. And each day gets better."

There were no half-lives here. Not for me or my kids or Rhodes.

"Can't tell you how glad I am to hear that. To know I'm the one who gets to give that to you."

I tipped my head up and pressed a kiss beneath his jaw. "And I hope I give it right back to you."

He tilted his head down, his lips meeting mine. "Every minute of every day, baby. And that's why I got you this."

He leaned to the side and reached into his pocket to pull something out. When he held his hand in front of me and opened it, revealing the most stunning ring I'd ever seen in all my life, all the air whooshed from my lungs.

"It's always been you, Blythe. It was you when I was seventeen. It was you for all those years we were apart, and it'll be you for the rest of my life. So what do you say? You want to do forever with me?"

My eyes welled up with happy tears as he slid the ring onto my left hand. Cupping his cheeks, I pulled his face to mine and kissed him with every ounce of love I felt for him. "There's no one else I'd want forever with."

# Epilogue

## Rhodes

*Sometime later*

This was happiness.

The sun on my skin, the comfortable breeze rustling the leaves of the trees, our family and closest friends watching on as I waited for the most important moment of my life.

For twenty years, I thought this day would never come. I thought I'd lost the only woman who would ever own me, heart and soul. Then the door opened and my whole world came stepping through.

At the first sight of my bride, my lungs seized and my heart swelled so big it took up every inch of space in my chest.

Nothing about my Angel was conventional, so it made perfect sense that her wedding dress would fit her personality. The silky fabric flowed around her legs in the breeze, the color reminding me of the Caribbean waters . . . of those perfect eyes, and I knew this was the moment I would take with me when I finally left this earth. This one right here. Watching my woman and our kids walk down the aisle to me so I could make us a family once and for all.

Avett wore a suit, looking dapper and mature as ever as he linked his elbow with his mother's, taking his job of walking her down the aisle very seriously.

Adeline and Ainsley wore miniature versions of their mom's dress as they walked a few feet in front, Koda right between them, tossing flower petals on the ground between the two columns of chairs.

A nickering sound from the newly built barn a few yards away caught Ainsley's attention, and she paused in her task to look in that direction. "Hi, Strawberry! Hi, Blaze! Hi, Fred!" she called out to the horses. Yes—*horses*. Blythe might have blown a gasket when I showed up with a trailer full of ginormous animals, but she eventually settled down. After all, she knew I was a sucker for those kids.

The crowd laughed at my baby girl's antics, and she

lapped it up, the little diva that she was. The girls reached me first, both of them latching on and hugging me with all their might.

I knelt down and wrapped them in my arms. "Love you both to the moon and back."

They returned the sentiment before placing kisses on my cheeks and skipping off to join Nona, Trick, and Tristan in the first row.

Avett and Blythe stopped in front of me, and I could see the emotion he was trying to hold back. It broke free and he lunged, his hug as tight as his sisters'. "Thank you for makin' us happy."

Christ, this kid was killing me. "It was an honor. You guys have my heart, forever and always."

He sniffled and nodded, turning to hug his mom before going to join his sisters.

"Angel," I breathed as she stepped up beside me.

Her smile lit up my whole goddamn world.

"Well, baby, what do you say?" she asked, reaching down to take my hand in hers. "You ready to do forever with me?"

Oh yeah. This was happiness.

And this was what it meant to live your very best life.

The End.

Thank you so much of reading!

*Keep going for a sneak peek of Nona and Trick's book,*
***THE BEST OF ME***

# Sneak Peek of The Best of Me

Want to know where Blythe got her start? Check out Nona and Trick's story, **THE BEST OF ME** now.

## Prologue

*Nona*

There were three things in life that I knew as absolute fact.

First, a good blowout and pretty undergarments could work wonders in boosting a woman's confidence.

Second, the shitty, worthless men outnumbered the good by about ten to two.

And finally, Emma Wanderly was a raging idiot.

That last one might have seemed harsh, but it was the stone-cold truth. After all, she didn't just have a *good* man. She had one of the very best.

And that idiot went and threw him away.

Seeing as I spent years upon years married to the scummiest, lowest form of man there was, I considered myself somewhat of an expert in the field of men, especially when it came to telling the good from the bad. So I knew to my bones that my take on Patrick "Trick" Wanderly was spot-on.

I'd see him and his family around town and wish I were lucky enough to have a man like that in my life. A man who didn't shy away from showing affection to his wife in public, letting her and everyone else around know just how much he loved her with nothing but a touch or caress or simply a look. A man who'd watch his kids and smile or shake his head good-naturedly, like he got a kick out of them acting like typical rowdy children.

He was a man content with all the blessings in his life and wasn't afraid to show it.

Don't get me wrong, my kids were absolutely everything to me, and each morning when they woke up and came stumbling into the kitchen, groggy and cranky with sleep, I knew just how lucky I was.

But in all our years of marriage, Christian had never looked at me or touched me the way Trick looked at and touched Emma. In public or in private. And for that reason, I couldn't help the twinge of jealousy that shot through my heart every time I saw them together.

Then, almost out of the blue, the picture-perfect couple was no more. I was baffled. Hell, all of Hope Valley was in a tizzy, struggling to figure out what had happened.

One second they seemed to have it all, and the next... *poof*. It was gone.

I didn't get it. Trick was sweet and incredibly kind. He was thoughtful, always putting others first. He was so funny I spent most of the time in his presence laughing until my stomach ached. And if all of that hadn't been enough, he was, hands down, the sexiest, most handsome man I'd ever laid eyes on.

Sandy brown hair clipped short in an easy-to-manage yet attractive style put his gorgeous features on display. A strong, square jaw that was always covered in a day's worth of light brown stubble, a straight, masculine nose, and eyes the most stunning gunmetal gray were only the tip of the iceberg that made Trick Wanderly all that he was. Broad shoulders led to a wide chest that eventually dipped into a trim waist. His strong arms were made to wrap around you and protect you from everything bad, and I'd fantasized about being in those arms more than was probably healthy.

It was those fantasies that made me turn around in the middle of a conversation I was having with friends and scan the massive crowd until my eyes finally found him. And the moment they did, my heart clenched so painfully it nearly stole my breath.

He looked miserable, heartbroken. *Devastated.* Like his whole world had been ripped out from beneath him.

I'd noticed that exact look on his face more times than I cared to count over the past months. A look he got whenever he thought no one would notice, or when he had too much on his mind and accidentally allowed that carefree mask to slip.

And every time I saw it, it broke my heart a little more.

I'd have given anything to be able to take that pain away from him, to heal those wounds. But I knew firsthand that it wasn't that easy. The best I could do was be there for him, offering a shoulder to lean on, an ear to listen, or a stiff drink when talking just wasn't going to cut it.

Offering my friends a distracted "I need a refill, be back," I found myself moving around the elegantly adorned tables beneath the canvas and twinkle lights of the romantic tent like I had tunnel vision.

I was halfway across the tent where Hayes and my girl Tempie were holding their wedding reception when Trick's head came up. It was almost as if he sensed me moving in his direction. Those beautiful gray eyes locked with mine and that sadness melted away, replaced with a smile that made my knees weak and my belly quiver.

My lips tipped up of their own accord, offering him a small grin in return, and the sway of my hips grew a little more pronounced as I closed the rest of the distance.

"Officer," I greeted teasingly.

The low, rich chuckle that rolled from his chest felt like a gift. "Darlin'," he returned. "You havin' a good time?"

"I am. Good food, good people, celebration. Makes for a great night."

That shadow slid over his face once more before he tamped it down. "I hear that."

"How about you?"

He knocked back the last of the amber liquid in his

glass and raised a finger to the bartender for another. As soon as his fresh drink was placed in front of him, he lifted it and slugged back half in one gulp, telling me what frame of mind he was in before he turned back to me with a smile that didn't even come close to meeting his eyes. "Yeah, sweetheart. I'm happy for them."

"Didn't ask if you were happy for them, honey," I murmured, leaning in close. "I asked if you were having a good time."

"Nona—" Just then, the band shifted from a fast tempo, peppy song to something slower and softer.

Curling my fingers around his big hand, I gave it a tug and commanded, "Come on, Officer. I'll let you take me for a spin on the floor."

He allowed me to pull him off his stool and lead him toward the makeshift dance floor, rolling his eyes playfully when I spun around and placed my free hand on his shoulder.

The small flutters I'd been feeling in my belly since his fingers closed around mine erupted the moment his large palm slid along my waist and settled on the small of my back. With Trick leading, we fell into an easy rhythm and moved in silence until I found the courage to say what I'd wanted to say since first approaching him.

"It gets easier," I murmured quietly. His eyes flashed to me, and I watched in panic as that beautiful gray grew intense and stormy. But the words were already out there, and there was no pulling them back.

*In for a penny, in for a pound, Nona,* I thought as I pulled in a steady breath.

"I won't tell you it gets better, but it does get easier. I promise, Trick."

Those clouds parted. His face went soft and sympathetic as he whispered, "Speaking from experience, darlin'?"

"You know I am," I replied sadly. There'd been no hiding it. The whole town knew about my failed marriage, and I was sure there were still rumblings going around about how stupid I'd been not to end it much sooner than I had. But I'd been in love, and when you loved someone so strongly that you built a life and a family together, throwing in the towel just wasn't that simple.

I'd made myself a promise when things started to turn from bad to worse. I was going to do whatever I could. I was going to fight and scratch and claw so *I knew* beyond the shadow of a doubt that I'd done everything in my power to make my marriage work. So when it was all said and done, I could hold my head up high, I could look at my kids and know I hadn't just given up when things got too hard.

Now it was over, and I spent every day with my head held high in the knowledge that I'd given it my all.

"Fuckin' idiot."

My chin jerked back and my eyes went wide at the venom in his voice. "Wh-what?"

"Christian Fanning," he answered, speaking my ex-husband's name in a rough, craggy growl. "Fuckin' idiot."

My head cocked to the side, and I felt my face go gentle as I looked up at him. "She's gonna hate herself," I whispered, and at my words, he closed his eyes as pain filtered across his handsome face.

"Nona—"

"She'll wake up one day and realize exactly what she lost. She'll realize she had it all and she just let it go, and she'll hate herself for it."

"Sweetheart—"

"You're an incredible man, Trick. Best man I've ever met."

The hand holding mine let go and came up, the pads of his fingers dragging gently along my cheekbone as he tucked my hair behind my ear. "That can't be true."

"It is," I declared forcefully. "Trust me, Trick. It's true. I know shitty men. I know lazy men. I know all about worthless pieces of shit who don't care about anything or anyone but themselves. And *you aren't that.*

You're amazing. And smart. And funny. And sexy—" My diatribe came to a screeching halt. I hadn't meant to say that last part out loud. Slamming my eyes closed, I hung my head in mortification as my cheeks caught fire.

He put pressure beneath my chin, forcing my head back up so he could see me. "Nona, darlin'."

I gave my head a shake. "Excuse me while I wait for the floor to open up and swallow me."

His body shook against mine, and I knew he was laughing, but I didn't find anything about this the slightest bit funny. "Come on, Nona. Open those pretty eyes for me." After a few more humiliating seconds, I peeled my eyelids open and nearly melted into a puddle at the warmth radiating from his gaze. "Means the world to me, honey, everything you just said. The absolute world."

"It's just... what I meant to say is I'm here, you know, if you ever need to talk. I get it... so I'm here. For you."

"You're pretty incredible yourself."

I lowered my eyes again as a fierce blush stole up my neck. "Thanks," I whispered shyly.

"And beautiful."

My head shot back up, my lips parting on a surprised inhale. "Th-thank you."

Something in his expression changed. It was as if he could suddenly read every thought in my head. The longing, the desire I'd felt for him for months. In an instant there was a flare of heat that hadn't been there just a moment before, so hot it turned the gray to liquid. The intensity of it made my knees buckle, and I would have hit the floor, embarrassing myself even further if it hadn't been for Trick's other arm banding around my waist and pulling me tight against him.

The look in his eyes was enough to make my breathing ragged as my heart pounded against my ribs.

"Trick," I panted as my breasts swelled and my nipples hardened.

"You wanna get outta here, sweetheart?"

I did. I *really* did. So I gave him a little nod and followed eagerly as he took my hand once more and led me from the dance floor and out of the tent, excitement coursing through my veins as I skipped to keep up.

A loud thump followed by a quietly hissed "Shit" startled me out of a dead sleep. I blinked my eyes as they slowly adjusted to the darkness surrounding me. My fuzzy brain had trouble recalling what was going on, but when I rolled toward the noise that had woken me, the twinge between my thighs was enough to bring the whole night back to me.

Trick dragging me from the wedding reception, loading me in his truck, and driving like a bat out of hell. The way his jagged voice abraded against my skin when he asked, "Your kids home?" and the soft breathiness of mine as I replied, "They're with their dad this weekend."

Everything that came after was completely and utterly out of this world. It was a dream come true. No, actually it was *better* than anything I could have dreamed up. *He* was better.

Trick Wanderly was the best lover I'd ever had—not that I had many to compare him to, but still. He'd fucked me hard and rough, he made love to me slow and gentle, he made me feel a million things I'd never felt before, and he spent hours doing it *thoroughly* until we both passed out from exhaustion.

My body ached in the most delectable ways from the workout he'd given it, and as I finished my roll, a smile spread across my face so wide my cheeks ached. That was, until I caught a glimpse of Trick's shadowed frame in the dark.

Twisting around quickly, I flicked on the lamp beside my bed and spun back to him. "What are you doing?"

He finished pulling up the tuxedo slacks he'd been

wearing before I slowly stripped him out of them hours earlier. His shirt was already on but unbuttoned, revealing tanned skin over ripped muscles from his chest all the way down to where that sexy V dipped into his waistband and the small smattering of hair sprinkled over his pecs. I'd never considered myself a fan of chest hair, but Trick's was minimal and *extremely* hot.

"I was gonna wake you."

My fingers clenched in the comforter, lifting it higher to cover my bare breasts as a chill rushed across my skin. "You were gonna wake me... what? Before you bailed out at—" I jerked around to look at my alarm clock. "—four fifteen in the morning?"

That chill turned biting when Trick blew out a deep sigh and dropped his head, reaching up to rub at the back of his neck. The Trick who'd looked at me on that dance floor in a way that made me tremble with desire was long gone. This Trick made my stomach churn while my throat threatened to close up.

"I'm sorry, darlin'," he started uncomfortably, making everything so much worse. "So damn sorry."

*I'm sorry.* Two words no woman wants to hear after sleeping with a man she's been crushing on for months and months.

"You're... sorry," I repeated, doing a slow blink as I stared up at him, feeling my heart shrivel up in my chest.

His head shot back up, those piercing gray eyes pinning me to the mattress as if he could hear the heartache in my voice. "I wasn't gonna sneak out, sweetheart. I'd never do that, not to you."

"But...?" I asked, because I just knew there was a *but* coming. I might not have wanted to hear it, but I needed to get this over with. Like ripping off a Band-Aid, swift and without hesitation so he could leave and I could curl up into a ball and have myself a good long breakdown in privacy.

"I shouldn't have done this."

Okay, that *killed*. Squeezing my eyes closed against the onslaught of tears burning my eyes, I turned my head away and pulled in a much-needed breath.

The mattress dipped a second later, and I felt the tips of his fingers under my jaw, turning my face back to his. With no other choice, I opened my eyes and realized I'd gotten it wrong. What I felt a few seconds ago hadn't killed. The guilt in those grays just then did. "I'm so, *so* sorry."

"You said that already," I croaked, my words thick with sadness.

"Because it's true," he responded softly. "You have to believe me, darlin'. I didn't realize I wasn't ready for this until—" He stopped, his throat bobbing with a hard swallow. "I thought I was there, that enough time had passed. You deserve better than what I can give you, Nona. I never would've gone there if—"

"God, please stop." I held my hand up to silence him as my face twisted in pain. His words so far had sliced into me deep enough; I didn't think I could handle anything more. "Just stop. I get it."

"Nona—"

"No, really," I cut in again, this time shoving my way off the bed with the sheet wrapped around me to hide my nakedness. "Like I said, I get it." I began frantically moving around the room, searching for my panties. "Your divorce was basically *just* finalized." I tagged them and struggled to get them up my legs without dropping the sheet. "I totally understand."

"Nona, please just—"

I shuffled toward my dresser, nearly tripping over my own feet. "I should've thought about that. I didn't mean to put you in such an awkward position." I got the drawer open and pulled out the first nightie my fingers landed on, somehow managing to get it over my head and down my body without flashing Trick.

"Sweetheart. If you'd just—"

Now fully clothed, I felt more equipped to handle the crushing blow of rejection he'd just landed. I whipped my hair out of my face and turned back to him, inhaling through my nose in an attempt to calm my frayed nerves.

"Please. Just go," I spoke, my voice weak and quiet, revealing the ache centered in my chest. "Please, Trick."

His face fell, and the sympathy in those stormy eyes nearly did me in. "I don't wanna leave things like this."

My head started bobbing on a nod. "Because you're an amazing man. But I'm asking you, please, just go."

I could see the struggle written all over his face. He didn't want to leave until he was certain I was okay. He was just that good of a guy. Problem was, I didn't think I'd be okay for a good long while, and I needed him *gone* so I could deal with everything I was feeling on my own.

He took a few steps closer, reaching up to place his hand on the side of my neck and brush his thumb across my jaw. As hard as it was—and it was agonizing—I managed to stay still and not flinch away as he took that last piece from me. "You know I care about you, right? That'll never change, Nona."

My head tilted of its own accord, pressing deeper into his touch. "I know." But that knowledge only made me feel worse.

Trick remained unmoving, his eyes scanning every inch of my face as something played across his features I couldn't even begin to understand. Then, with a gentle, sad smile, he finally dropped his arm, turned to gather the rest of his stuff, and moved out of my room.

I heard the front door close seconds later, and with it, the first tear fell.

## **Chapter 1**

*Nona*

*A month and a half later*

"Yes! That's it, baby, that's it! You got this!" I shot from my chair as my son, Tristan, faked left, dribbling the soccer ball down the field. "Yes! Go, Tris! Take the shot!"

And he did, kicking the ball with everything he had, sending it sailing past the goalie and scoring another point for his team, putting them in the lead.

Throwing my hands in the air, I jumped up and down and shouted out my excitement, high-fiving a bunch of the other moms crowded around me on the side of the field before turning back and yelling, "You're awesome, baby!"

My kid looked in my direction as he jogged back to the center of the field, his expression a mixture of embarrassment and excitement as he gave me a low wave while getting claps on the back and shoulders from his teammates.

"Attaboy, Tristan! Keep it up!" My head turned at the deep, masculine rumble coming from down the field before I could stop it.

For a month and a half, I'd done everything I could to avoid Trick Wanderly like my life depended on it. Unfortunately, avoiding the man I'd spent one amazing night with was proving to be hard in a small town like ours.

Trick's head turned, those gunmetal eyes met mine, and I watched with my heart throbbing as his face grew soft and his lips tilted up into a grin.

I offered a small, polite wave and looked away, my attention moving toward the small cluster of women sitting across the field near our team's goal. Emma Wanderly sat in the middle of the gaggle, the Queen Bee of what I referred to as the Stylish Soccer Moms. The ones who always dressed like they were either coming from or heading to yoga but managed to make it look über stylish in ways I couldn't comprehend. The ones whose makeup always looked flawless even with the sun beating down on them. The ones with the big Louis Vuitton or Michael Kors totes filled with snacks for the kiddos like carrot sticks or apples, celery sticks with peanut butter and raisins—something you just *knew* was super healthy.

Meanwhile, I was wearing a pair of jeans that fit tight to my ass, so battered there was a slit in one knee and a hole on my left thigh close to the pocket. My ribbed tank was faded, but you could still clearly read the black block letters on the front that declared "I came. I saw. I made it awkward." My own off-brand handbag contained a mini bag of Cheetos, another of nacho cheese Doritos, and a pack of fruit snacks. My face was free of makeup, and after spending the entire week working on other women's hair, the last thing I wanted to do was screw with mine, so my long red locks were currently thrown up in a messy ponytail.

I put in effort during the week when it came to my appearance, but unless I was going out with my girls, the weekends were mine, and it was all about relaxing and taking a load off, not dolling up for no damn good reason.

Emma didn't hoot or holler when her son scored a goal. She simply clapped and smiled her brilliant white smile, always behaving with class and decorum.

In other words, she was my polar opposite, and it was no wonder Trick regretted hooking up with me when he'd spent years with a woman like her.

My focus drifted a couple yards down from Emma, where their oldest, a girl named Hannah, was hanging with a couple kids who looked around her age. As I studied her, I couldn't help but think what I thought every time I saw Hannah Wanderly. She was the spitting image of her father, only female. And Trick made a *gorgeous* girl. There wasn't a doubt in my mind that he was living a nightmare with a teenaged daughter that beautiful.

It was on that thought that I felt an odd sensation prickle across my skin. As hard as I tried to fight it, my head turned back in the direction of Trick, and I found him watching me with a look on his face that, in spite of the warm, sunny day, made goose bumps break out along my arms.

I felt that gaze like a physical touch as he scanned from my behind back up to my face, and that grin of his returned once more.

"Shit," I mumbled under my breath, jerking my attention back to the field.

Tristan had control of the ball again but didn't have a shot at the goal, so he passed it to a teammate who was open. That boy took the shot, but it went a little wide, missing the goal by inches, and a man a few feet away immediately shot to his feet, his face red and pinched in a way I knew wasn't good.

"Damn it, Cal! Get your head in the game!" he shouted toward the boy who'd just missed. I tensed as the other parents all turned to look at the man, but my focus was on the boy as his dad continued to berate him. "You were wide open, for Christ's sake! Stop screwin' around and focus!"

I could see the anxiety rolling off the poor kid from where I stood, and the longer the man shouted the more wired the boy got, until he was locked so tight he totally screwed up the next play, going for a kick and missing the ball altogether.

"Are you kidding me!" the man hollered, yanking off his baseball cap and stomping up to the edge of the field. "I didn't shell out cash for this damn league so you could embarrass me, boy! Focus or get off the freakin' field!"

That was when I'd officially had enough. "Hey!" At my shout, the man quit castigating his kid and moved his angry eyes to me. "How about you lay off, huh? You're only making it worse."

"How 'bout you mind your own business?"

This guy was really starting to piss me off, so I planted my hands on my hips and turned my body fully toward him. "They're eleven and twelve, man. This isn't a professional club, so just cool it."

"You handle your son and I'll handle mine," he spat. "Like I said, none of your damn business."

"Dude, you made it my business when you started shouting so loud the heavens could hear you, takin' a tone I'm not particularly fond of you using in front of my kid."

The asshole looked me up and down with an ugly sneer, lowering his voice enough that the kids couldn't hear as he declared, "No wonder your man stepped out before finally getting shot of your ass. Had a naggin' bitch like you at home, I'd bail out too."

I barely had time to register the sting that caused before the air around us shifted.

"You're gone. Right now."

Turning woodenly, I looked to see Trick was no longer down the field but at my back, only inches away, and he was staring at the guy who'd just insulted me like it was taking all his strength not to rip the asshole's head off.

The guy's frame jerked back at the venom in Trick's voice. "'Scuse me?"

"You heard me," Trick continued on a growl so vicious it sent a shiver down my spine. "You wanna watch the rest of the game, you do it from your car. But you aren't here."

The man blustered, his chest puffing out and stretching the shirt that was already taxed from his beer gut that much tighter. "You got no right—"

"Don't know you, man, but know *of* you. Which means you at least know of me, so you know I got a badge. That means I have every right. You're disturbing the peace, so you have five seconds to get gone."

The asshole's face grew ruddy. "I'm not disturbin' a damn thing."

"My peace was most definitely disturbed," June Hiller declared. I knew June relatively well. Her son had played on the same team as mine the past four years, and I liked her a lot. She wasn't part of the Stylish Soccer Moms club. She was my kind of people.

"I'm disturbed too," another dad chimed in, looking nearly as pissed as Trick. "On behalf of my kid, his kid, *and* Ms. Fanning. And just to say, this jerkoff doesn't get lost soon, things are gonna go downhill fast. No man worth his salt talks to a woman like that."

"You can't just—"

"That's where you're wrong," Trick cut in. "I can and I just did. Now you only got five seconds to get to your car and away from this field. And I catch you shoutin' at any more games or even get word you took your shit out on your kid when you get home, I'll be payin' you a visit. And trust me, man, you do *not* want that."

He stuttered over a few words, his ruddy cheeks growing purple with rage and what I expected was a great deal of humiliation, before finally wising up, spinning around, and stomping off to his car.

"Hey." At Trick's soft voice and the feel of his fingers wrapping gently around my wrist, I turned from watching the jackass back to him. "You okay, darlin'?"

I stared up at him with my lips parted. "I, uh...."

His forehead pulled into a frown as he used his grip on my wrist to tug me even closer. "Don't you give what that asshole said a second thought, Nona. He was full of shit."

That got a response out of me, but not the one either of us had been expecting. "You really shouldn't cuss. Not, like, in general," I added quickly. "Just, you know... here. Around a bunch of kids."

He looked to the field and back to me, smiling and dropping his voice as he said, "Wasn't speaking loud, sweetheart. Think it's safe to say they couldn't hear me."

I lifted a shoulder in a tiny shrug. "Still."

"I hear you, and I'll be mindful from here on out. But you still haven't answered my question."

He was too close. He smelled too good. And he was way too damn handsome. This was *not* good. Struggling to clear the Trick-induced haze from my brain, I pinched my brows together and asked, "Um... sorry. Wh-what was your question?"

"You okay after what that a—jerk said to you?"

"Oh, yeah. No, I'm good." I waved my free hand

between us. "Believe me, a guy like *that* isn't gonna get my hackles up."

His fingers clenched, pressing deeper into the sensitive skin beneath my wrist. "You sure? What he said—"

I wrenched my hand free, trying not to make it seem too obvious I couldn't handle his touch. "Trust me. I'm fine. Yeah, it stung, I'll give you that, but it won't last. What Chris did isn't on me."

"That's right, darlin'."

And that right there was why I needed to avoid Trick for my own damn good. That soft look, that sweet smile. For crying out loud, I could still recall how he felt and tasted like it hadn't been a month and a half ago but only a few hours. Thankfully the referee blew the whistle, calling the end of the game, and I was able to take a step back and break the weird intensity swirling between us.

Something from the corner of my eye caught my attention, and I looked over to see Emma staring lasers at me from all the way across the field, her arms crossed over her chest and her face twisted in displeasure.

*Oh shit.*

"Mom! Mom!" Tristan came running up to me, his face ruddy and his hair slicked with sweat. "I scored a goal and we won!"

I smiled at him, loving that my kid hadn't hit that

dreaded phase yet where just my presence embarrassed him. He was twelve, so it was only a matter of time, but I was going to lap it up while it lasted. Grabbing Tristan's shoulder, I pulled him into my side and gave him a quick one-armed hug. "I saw that, sweetie. You totally rocked it!"

"I totally did." His eyes shifted from me to Trick, who was still standing close. "Hey, Mr. Wanderly."

"Hey, bud. You were awesome out there. That goal was a thing of beauty."

A second later, Trick's son Shawn came running up, offering his father a "Hi Dad" before reaching up to bump Trick's fist with his own.

"Hey Shawn. Great game."

Shawn looked at me with a smile just like his dad's. "Thanks Ms. Nona."

Tristan spun on me, bouncing with excitement and leftover adrenaline from his win before asking, "Can I go over to Shawn's to play video game? Please?"

"Oh, uh...." I looked between all three sets of male eyes, wondering how my life had gotten so freaking twisted up. "I'm sure his mom has plans, babe."

"We're with Dad this weekend," Shawn interjected. "And he'd totally be cool with it!" He looked to Trick for the second time since joining our huddle. "Right Dad? You're cool if Tris comes over, right?"

"Tris, baby. I'm sure—"

"Fine by me," Trick cut in before I could finish my objection and get the hell out of there. I needed a big glass of wine, stat. "That is," he continued, his gray eyes boring into me, "if it's cool with you."

*Well damn.* It would appear he'd decided he wasn't going to make my avoidance easy. "Well... okay. Yeah. I guess it's okay."

"I'm gonna stop off somewhere to grab the kids a bite if you wanna come with."

There was no way that was going to happen. Standing here with him was hard enough, remembering what it was like to have exactly what I'd wanted—him— but having it ripped away only hours later. Lunch was out of the question.

"Thanks, but I've got some errands I have to run. But I can swing by and get him on my way home later."

His expression gentled as he said, "You don't need to worry about that, sweetheart. I'll bring him back to you later."

Trick in my house... again... for the first time since... well, *that night.* "You sure? I don't mind—"

"I'm sure." God, I really needed him to quit being so wonderful. It was killing me. "I'll text you when we're on the way over. That work?"

"Yeah, that'll work." I shifted back to Tristan and

gave his shoulder a little jostle, not going in for the full hug I wanted since his friend was standing right there. "You behave, yeah? Do as Mr. Wanderly says."

"Got it, Mom."

"You sure you don't wanna join us?" Trick asked again.

"I'm good. But thanks for asking. I should get back home to Blythe. She was still crashed when we left the house. I should probably make sure my girl doesn't sleep the whole day away." Giving Tris one last squeeze, I started backing up, blowing him a kiss since I knew I wouldn't get away with a real one. "See you soon, bud. Be good and love you."

"Yeah Mom. Love you too."

Then, with one last wave, I turned on my flip-flops and bolted. It might have seemed cowardly, but I was just fine with that.

CLICK HERE TO KEEP READING

# Jessica's Princesses

Come be a part of Jessica's Princesses Reader Group, where you'll get first looks at cover reveals, what's coming next, and so much more.

Jessica's Princesses

# About Jessica

Born and raised around Houston, Jessica is a self proclaimed caffeine addict, connoisseur of inexpensive wine, and the worst driver in the state of Texas. In addition to being all of these things, she's first and foremost a wife and mom.

Growing up, she shared her mom and grandmother's

love of reading. But where they leaned toward murder mysteries, Jessica was obsessed with all things romance.

When she's not nose deep in her next manuscript, you can usually find her with her kindle in hand.

Connect with Jessica now

www.authorjessicaprince.com

Jessica's Princesses Reader Group

Newsletter

Instagram

Facebook

TikTok

authorjessicaprince@gmail.com

www.ingramcontent.com/pod-product-compliance
Lightning Source LLC
Chambersburg PA
CBHW061113310726
48974CB00002B/518